DEMONS

DEMONS

SEAD
MAHMUTEFENDIĆ

Demons

Copyright © 2024 by Sead Mahmutefendic. All rights reserved.

No part of this publication may be reproduced, stored in a retrieval system or transmitted in any way by any means, electronic, mechanical, photocopy, recording or otherwise without the prior permission of the author except as provided by USA copyright law.

The opinions expressed by the author are not necessarily those of URLink Print and Media.

1603 Capitol Ave., Suite 310 Cheyenne, Wyoming USA 82001
1-888-980-6523 | admin@urlinkpublishing.com

URLink Print and Media is committed to excellence in the publishing industry.

Book design copyright © 2024 by URLink Print and Media. All rights reserved.

Published in the United States of America

Library of Congress Control Number: 2024922710
ISBN 978-1-68486-968-8 (Paperback)
ISBN 978-1-68486-973-2 (Digital)

16.10.24

For those who believe that man cannot be guilty. Who can bear responsibility for what is beyond one's power? For man is, after all, a weak, unreliable and guiltless creature governed by secrets and evil forces that he, most often, is not even aware of, which is why he invented guilt as an alibi for his vast and fatal ignorance and stupidity. Human life is a constant sense of shame before all those dead souls, whose tired blood we bear and curse.

I

THE SOULS OF CHILDREN AND SINNERS BELONG TO HEAVEN. THE FORMER DIDN'T HAVE TIME TO SIN, AND THE LATTER ARE HERETICS. THAT'S THAT, JUST SO YOU KNOW.

You are probably familiar from the newspapers with the case of Albert Wollensky, who, shortly after seeing the capital city, went to a monastery, but when it turned out that the monks there were mostly former residents of the capital, he had no choice but to bid farewell to asceticism and abstinence, and to settle in a small town in the interior, where he was soon appointed as a professor of French and Latin at the local high school.

Let me get straight to the point: that, indeed, is my case, as I am the aforementioned Albert Wollensky. As I sit in front of a blank piece of paper, as if in front of my temptation and challenge, whilst at the moment of being aware that I will soon have to face myself, the question indeed arises in me what kind of sense, first of all, can this story of mine make, even if it were the sincerest one? Who needs it except, perhaps, me? What is the purpose of waving the rags of my past life like a battle flag, which I insist on keeping upright at any cost, even though defeat is already quite certain?

And what if it is precisely the one least needed by me, not to mention of any use?

The mentioned capital dwellers probably believed they had to escape their city by committing suicide; one after another, they were dying of typical metropolitan arrogance; I guess they didn't know that there existed small places where one could gossip just as nicely, perhaps even more nicely, whine just as much, maybe even more fiercely and convincingly, recount stories more seductively, in private and behind closed doors, where one loves a little and even more passionately hates, but most of all where scheming prevails all with extreme and meticulous passion, which would eventually exhaust even a horse.

Having a pen, plenty of paper, some patience and far more cool wits, a strong stomach, balls of steel, the devil's message that everything is pointless, and above all the feeling that our life is nothing more than the most ordinary trick for the gullible and a trap not worth attaching more significance than the one of not being hungry or thirsty and having a place to get a good sleep, nor should one hold one's head down before it, nor this story, which I hope to write to the end only because I cannot see myself having anything better to do, and, of course, if my patience doesn't fail me.

As human life is subject to oblivion, as events that occur in time are lost along with it, I find it worthwhile to endeavor that events, especially those that attempt to shed light on my actions and my soul caused by the past, do not remain in darkness, but rather be documented in writing for those who will be more deeply interested in my case and thus become more widely known. For this reason, to all who in the future will be willing to acquaint themselves with what follows, I declare the following: I am not justifying myself before anyone, let it be known. Henceforth, I expect no benefit for myself. I am sad, for as long as I can remember, I have always been alone, and thus, I accept loneliness and rejection as my given fate. I know what I deserve, so I am prepared for my action to drive me out of this life soon, although even today, I wouldn't be certain in claiming that it is ugly and inhumane. Life is beautiful, only the people in it are less so. The souls of the dead are far more beautiful than those of the living. The latter, of course, does not refer to the common and everyday sense that people take each other's lives, but is, first of all, a sad picture of our metaphysical nature, which, well, I failed to resist, and indeed, did not particularly even bother to resist. Quite frankly. Fair and square.

What society will most likely do to me will be more of retribution and revenge than an adequate weighing of what I have done to some of its innocent and virtuous figures. Pity or, indeed, forgiveness from the jury would degrade me as much as the sincerity in this story of mine; of course, if I allow myself that. Only then will I be myself because I have long believed I have reached such freedom of spirit where I do not expect anything from anyone and where the perfect indifference reigns in my soul. The only remaining fact is that I regret being born at all, but that was not my decision, but the will of others, and therefore, I really cannot do anything about it or bear someone else's responsibility. It was probably worth seeing some things even for a moment rather than being forever sealed in darkness to be picked up by some force. It feels as if I am still dreaming a strange dream in which I see myself alive just until the real Albert wakes up. Roughly, something like a dream within a dream. This happens too: I catch myself as if waiting for something or someone, say, for someone to shake me by the shoulder, wake me up and say to me while still drowsy, "You dreamed all of that."

At the moment when I begin this story, I am still in a dilemma whether to veil my confession with parody or to have it as yet another proof of how much I do not understand what is happening before my eyes. My life has nothing to do with a joke; things got serious long ago. So, what should I do? Should I succumb to the coldness regarding my feelings, which will necessarily require a certain distress, which again is more of a false ploy out of anger and revenge than a sincere desire not to touch what might be false modesty.

I would be happy if this record of mine, this word of mine about souls in mortal agony, is read by at least someone, although I do not believe, nor is it in my nature to believe that anything can be explained by it.

Why do I write then? Where do such need and illusion for so many words still come from, which will, at best, remain for someone's amusement and distraction? Is one bullet more valuable than a pile of words? Ah, who knows? The bullet is there to relieve a man of the tension imposed by others, and the word is there to illuminate, or at least to try to illuminate. Anger ignites the word, while the word soothes the torment and casts a spell over it. Finally, the only truth is that they are all one and that they imitate each other.

I can barely recall the details that undoubtedly serve to indicate or hint at certain answers, which, at the moment of writing this, I still do not foresee, and which quite frankly I neither need, nor can they any longer help me. I am left to seek comfort in them, for they are the only ones that can give me malicious satisfaction, which will mostly be limited by frivolity and the summoning of painful memories why torment my spirit so much and in such a way when the sleepless nights have already tormented it enough? Besides, there are also fragments of conversations that reveal all our loneliness, sighs, unfortunate and foolish decisions when we are alone with ourselves and when one secretly squeezes the other's hand.

I search, search, sit, dig, sense, reminisce, struggle. Where to find the right words and wherefrom do I get such powerful words for what I remember happened, which I confide to myself. Sometimes I don't even hesitate to speak about it out loud, let alone confide anything to someone else. It seems to me that all the breath could leave me at that moment. Then I usually say that I have a good friend, lonely and unhappy as I am (friends are usually lonely and unhappy like us), who told me this and that, and then cautiously reveal his confession, and dread that the one sitting across from me does not realize that it is, in fact, our common sorrow.

Lately, I have no desire for any game. I have no desire to seek an alibi before myself. I want to see myself as I am, without makeup and a mask, for my soul has remained the last station at which I disembarked a long time ago, tired of this journey called life. It is the last institution I still care about a little, although I do not feel it quite seriously, as it is, after all, with many people, that at the moment when the time for a terrible confrontation approaches, they flee from themselves like the devil from the cross; on the contrary, I call for it and wish it to happen as soon as possible so that everything finally becomes indifferent to me. Thus, I take the liberty of stating that a good part of my honorable intention inevitably gets covered with a painted hypocrisy. Therefore, I will have to return to my earlier feelings, if I haven't already misplaced them somewhere, because if I fail, it will all be a futile job without meaning, without significance, just as sorrow and our anger are meaningless if stripped of their aura of grandeur, ignoring the fact that it is mere draining of tear ducts in the eyes and a physiological release of overstrained nerves.

I will follow myself through time which is kind to no one, myself included, but it is significant insofar as it reflects itself through us. I strive for people who will hope fully not be the same after I finish this story of mine. They will remain as real as they were when I was with them, so real that they will be more real than their real selves; they will be far more serious witnesses in memory than they were when they were alive. Understandably, I will not be able to avoid praise and reproach, but if I shamelessly and grumpily treat them and hide behind the true reality approval of what I did, in that case, my words will have to find themselves in a situation where they can no longer enjoy serious respect, and my actions, among other things, will be despised as cunning, treacherous and shallow, and perhaps even less than that.

I write this confession of mine as a bad joke. I admit that it has already taken on a serious and even enigmatic form within me for which I must still sit down and strive to convince myself or someone else that it is not, after all, just my bad joke. My goal is to ascertain everything I have observed, naturally, if it does not dispute the one who lives, works, suffers, and rejoices, and that it is not indifference, apathy, and ignorance in trying to understand the other, even if it seems painful, illogical, and unimaginable. The boldness to dive in and bitterly rebuke oneself, and the need for ridicule, primarily of oneself, and then of all other seemingly sacred things, will transform my words and turn them into sinful ones, although there has never been any sin, because the concept of sin cannot be established by the one who committed it, and even less by the one who did not commit it nor knows how to commit it, nor dares to commit it. Regarding this, I must note that I only believed those who renounced their wealth for the sake of modesty, and never "the modest" because they cannot be wealthy. The greatest thing in life is to be able but not to want. Only then can you sit across from God and play the card as an equal partner.

II

WITHOUT A TRACE. THE TRACE EXISTS, BUT IS INVISIBLE. TO FIND SALVATION FOR THE SOUL

I rarely dream. If I were to count all my dreams, I could fit them on the fingers of one hand. Most often, I don't dream at all. For people like me, they say that we sleep like logs. I wouldn't dare to agree with such a statement, but let's say I sleep well, and thank God for that. Adding to this the fact that I also have a good appetite, following the famous principle of eat little, eat often! and that I have bowel movements about four to five times a day; last summer in July, on the twentieth, I went to the bathroom six times. All in all, I can say that I am a healthy man. And who is healthy let's be honest is also satisfied, and a satisfied person is indeed beneficial to society. Our nation is a wonderful nation, and every wonderful nation has its own wisdom expressed through proverbs. Nothing without folk wisdom. The folk say: he who is not satisfied with himself cannot be satisfied with others. They say: God made a beard for himself first, or: he who takes no care of himself, cannot take care of others. How simple, and yet so much wisdom is packed into those few words. Deep and above all wise, as wise as it gets.

Anyway, let me not get off track.

I had a strange dream. I wouldn't say it was entirely strange; but in some way, it was. Perhaps it is strange, if you look at it from one side, but if you look at it from the other side, it might not seem so strange. Still, I've somehow made this quite complicated, so I must go back a bit and remind myself of what I said a moment ago.

It rarely happens that I dream. If all my dreams were summed up, I do not believe that they could be counted on the fingers of both hands, although I mentioned just one a moment ago. I am a man who very, very rarely dreams, most often nothing. For people like me, it is customary to say that they sleep like logs. Like logs, as logs, I suppose that's how the saying goes. They have no problems troubling them, nor anything weighing on their minds during the day. That's what science says; there's nothing to add or subtract period.

I cannot agree with such thinking. It seems to me that I am precisely a person who has plenty of headaches about what I think and imagine. No one knows this except me. I believe it would be much easier for me if someone would honor me by hearing me out, even if they didn't approve of my everyday life. But let me not deviate from what I started a moment ago: about the dream. True, I haven't said anything specific about what I dreamt, but only stated the fact that I dream little, and that is precisely what troubles me the most. Where are my dreams, and how and why do they run away from me? Do I consciously stifle them and chase them away like a ghost that I won't be able to control as I do when I'm awake? I don't think that's not as important as my interest in whether I could see myself in a dream with the same eyes as I would like someone to see me; I said earlier, to at least hear me out, if one is not ready to justify me on the assumption that one cannot forgive me. But that is a completely different matter since it is a matter of forgiveness. I think that the only one who forgives is the one who wants to redeem oneself, justify oneself, or feel sorry for oneself.

I said, even though I rarely dream, quite rarely, I hold on dearly to what my dream presents because it tells me about its real power and its strange effect that, of course, concerns me and my life. I have never succeeded, though I have tried, to distance myself from it in a certain way, considering it as something that exists separately and independently from me, and to some extent, to dismiss it with contempt as a kind of superstition and self-deception, about which my sister Tereza had a very clear and categorical opinion that it has nothing to do with what a person thinks or sees during the day. I tried to somehow persuade and convince her, of course, while I still believed that she could mull over what she already had an irrefutable opinion on, but I soon had to give up, because not only did she not want to discuss it with me but, with a few trite phrases fed to her during political courses in dialectics and historical materialism, she started convincing me that I was a mystic and a man slightly detached from life and its practice, that I was beginning to lose touch with reality, and that I was imagining things which no one else saw but me, and that she was my sister and wanted to help me as her only brother, and we know, my dear Albert, where mysticism can lead a man. Religion, opium I heard her mention these two famous words.

But, Tereza dear, I have absolutely no interest in politics! I nervously wailed at her. I am interested in philosophy... the soul, metaphysics, transcendence. We know that every ideology, every doctrine has messed up its philosophy, if it even had one at all.

While I held my nerve, I nodded and with a certain smirk followed what she was dinning into my ear, which was neither nice nor polite, nor fair of me, and I would even dare to say that it was somewhat aggressive and condescending on my part, which could not possibly do me credit in such matters as the clash of opposing views. I can only imagine how both of us treated each other with some sort of arrogance, just as parents often do with their children whom they love because they are theirs, even though they babble incoherent and notorious nonsense, which could one day easily become "fatal".

Well, I happily recall that both of us, while we still had nerves for each other, nodded humoristically and fatalistically with the smile of someone more experienced, and somewhat desperate that we could not convince each other of our point of view, which was as clear as day to anyone who wanted to think a little or, if they could not understand, at least have a speck of tolerance. Neither of us showed any eagerness for it. Yes, I think that my sister Tereza and I used to opinionate just like that and behave in a mutually pugnacious manner. Today, no one persuades or dissuades anyone anymore, we live together under the same roof without one trying to mess with the other. The two of us can only talk about prices, expensiveness, who of the famous people has died recently, the water heater, and not for long because, after all, we would somehow manage to shift from the ordinary water heater wires to physics, and from physics to metaphysics and, in no time, we would have a debate about my mysticism.

However, no one even mentioned that word, to which I had already become so sensitive that, when reproached for it, I felt like ants were crawling up my body. "How can you say that?" I objected to her on one occasion. "It's similar to calling someone crazy just because they are different from you, while they, on the other hand, tolerates your "craziness" without ever calling it out, let alone reproaching you for it."

Let's return once again to my dreams. I, therefore, recorded each of my dreams. Just in case, pencil and paper were always there, within reach if I needed to write something down. It was usually a bunch of nouns into which I would occasionally insert a few verbs and adjectives to syntactically and logically link them into a whole so that the impressions from the dream, jumbled as they were higgledy piggledy would be completely clear when I read them later, better yet, to bring me back to that dream atmosphere or at least make me feel longing.

Lately, my experience, which I found in what I read, though strictly selected, began to rapidly expand so that the range between what I had known and held to be credible and what I adopted from reading quickly stood out and convinced me even more that life and the world could most reliably be interpreted by the insights I emphasized within myself. At the same time, I claimed that this was essential if certain secrets were to be interpreted, and the analytical debate I began to have with myself only reinforced that I was on the right path. It was something distinctly evident, which some may never see even in their dreams.

So, despite the fact that no one understood me, I diligently continued studying not only the essence of dreams but also their form, which I considered to be important if not more important than the first matter. But to say it all, I must finally recount what appeared to me in the dream and to which my sister Tereza again reacted with mockery and casually waved her hand after she had pitied me, granting me her attention and affection by listening to my story to the end; then suddenly, like a psychiatrist facing a hopeless case, she placed her hand on mine, smiled, and asked if I really cared that much about my dream so as to tell her about it and draw certain conclusions, which she already considered... you know what, my dear Albert, or if I was so bored that I had nothing better to do than to tell her my dreams, which were the most ordinary nightmares and fantasies. You know? If there's no one to listen to me, she will do her best to find someone similar to me and, what's more, with nerves of steel.

Well, even with the two of them her and my father the tap in the kitchen constantly drips, and everyone knows how expensive water is today, and even those metal bars for towels in the bathroom could use a bit of tightening because they could fall off any moment and chip the plaster from the wall.

I had long entertained the thought and secretly hoped of mocking such trivialities, especially if one unnecessarily and needlessly cudgels one's brains about them, and there are so many more important things to solve on this unfortunate planet, such as hunger, disease, and even the problem of alienation, which are constantly set aside for some more convenient and happier occasion, because well a screw can fall out at any moment and the plaster break off the wall, so it must be tightened with a screwdriver as soon as possible. You perceive the cry of a man as the whine of the whole mechanism that needs to be oiled, and things will happily go on. But I think, and not only do I think but I am also convinced that, in terms of tools, not only do I not have a screwdriver, but neither have I a hammer nor pliers; I would dare to say that I don't have a single nail of any size. If I had a screwdriver, sister Tereza, I would be a master craftsman. I tried to joke, but I instantly realized that it couldn't be a joke, but the most ordinary farce.

I think you are a genius said sister Tereza coldly, as coldly as she could say it, after which I realized that I had indeed gone too far with irony at the expense of those I did not particularly care for. It is rare that I forget myself and carelessly babble, that is, show off my big mouth. I could also count such instances on the fingers of one hand. The real things and the real me I mostly kept to myself, to think about them secretly, which was quite different from how I presented myself to others. My word and my thought often differed from each other, and not infrequentlyfully diametrically. Quite superficial listeners of what I said and emphasized with a subdued voice and intonation, that I often found myself having to repeat what I quietly and measuredly pronounced in the pose of a priest delivering a sermon with fingers spread and precisely pressed against the fingertips of the other hand, used to indiscreetly notice how I presented everything in a humorous and entertaining way, so it was always a true pleasure for them to listen to me, and even to learn whatever the topic was. In truth, I did not completely defend myself from these exaggerated compliments directed at my wit, loquacity, and the way I delivered it, but I must admit that most often, upon parting, I would feel miserable and empty, as if I had once again managed to betray myself because I was thinking more, or better say, trying to think and see the world through their eyes rather than how I see it, and well, God knows why I did not dare to say it. Let's lie again that I was hiding my misunderstood "self" from them.

Oh, God!

Last night too, (what devil compelled me to do that?), I dared to do something like that and told them about my dream, which had not given me peace for days. Tereza was sitting on my left. She kept nudging me with her foot as a sign to stop driveling on, and I, out of pure shame that someone of those present might notice that I was unable to finish the story my way, did not want to stop halfway so that, again, no one would suspect that I had probably received some kind of signal from someone to stop driveling on. I kept talking and saying what until then I had only trusted myself with.

I must admit that on several occasions I wanted to give my story a more casual and innocent tone, but that same devil whispered to me that now, since I had completely come out of hiding and discarded all caution, it was a great opportunity to let them know who I was and what I thought, and how and what I thought about. Let it be known, let those conceited and hollow noggins ponder. Let them gossip about me, let them.

The more I delved into the realm of the banal, the more I disturbed their peace, especially the peace of mind of my unfortunate sister, who, the very same evening, after the guests, so bewildered and confused, had dispersed and she had escorted them one by one in the foyer, holding their coats and smiling absent-mindedly at every one of them, and they responded with whole salvos of Anglo Saxon fake smiles, thus, that same evening, as soon as she returned from seeing off the last guest, closed the zipper on her smiling lips to give her face its natural expression. She then unleashed another kind of salvo at me, this time not quite so kindly: "Listen, you… what should I call you? she angrily pointed her index finger at me, "you… whatever you are?… it doesn't even matter… do you know that you were committing mental terror on all those people, and I can no longer guarantee that I will ever see any of those dear and kind people who listened with utter stoicism to your bullshit and ramblings tonight, nor can I be sure that they will be able to restrain themselves from the entirely natural reaction that in this house they were listening to a one-hundred-and-fifty-percent idiot. Yes, an idiot, not at all – a madman. Madness is sheer intelligence for an idiot, you idiot! I already knew you had a loose screw, but only tonight did I realize that you are a total idiot. Oh well!"

III

DIALOGUE OF THE SOUL WITH THE BODY OF THE DECEASED

Well, you see, while we're on the subject, I would venture to tell you about that dream. It is enough for me to recall it and right away, instantly, I shudder and with a heavy heart recount how in it continued what actually happened to me in reality a little over a month ago, when I met my mother on the street. To make the matter complete and interesting, that very day was the eighteenth anniversary of the unfortunate woman's death. Eighteen years have just passed. In any case, it would have been absurd to pretend that I had not noticed her. God forbid! Absolutely not that, although I must mention this I could have easily turned my head away and proceeded as if I had not seen anything, had I at least adhered to the principle that the dead can never come back to life.

Again, I was a man in whom one could have absolute trust: by no means did I want to give her the impression that this fact confused me. The fact of again seeing my other alive in front of me, my mother who died exactly eighteen years ago, and on top of that, in the same blue muslin dress in which I last saw her when she blew me a kiss through the air from the window. She could do such a thing only because she knew she would soon be deceased, and I guess, that is why she smiled at me so enigmatically, much like she used to smile at me from the window of the train she often used to take visiting her relatives in the capital together with my sister, who now does not even want to hear the story of this dream of mine.

After her death, no one explained anything to me that could be related to her, so I had to live for some time with certain assumptions that constantly intruded upon me in my reveries. I counted on the possibility that she would still come back, sooner or later, and that she would explain to me some of my doubts that had begun to seriously absorb me over time, considering also the fact that over time I realized my role in living with my mother was not entirely insignificant in character. I guess she must have known that too, as she often showered me with her affection, which caused a true explosion of satisfaction and happiness in me.

Under no circumstances did I want to let her down both for my own sense of security and the feeling that someone loved me, and from my own conviction that I could give myself to someone without reservation, and with excited passion.

When our eyes met, the first thing I noticed was that we were both extremely shaken, which could be easily seen on our faces, but actually, it would be more accurate to say that the real truth lay in the fact that we were both so surprised to see each other after several years that I had to, if only for a moment, wonder how is she here when she has long been dead? I believe she must have thought something similar because her smile was somewhat oblivious and a bit absent-minded. Even so, I cannot help but believe that it was more a consequence of the fear that our encounter would be brief, or... (I'll say this too)... perhaps she couldn't believe her eyes seeing that I was still among the living, and I was more inclined to take that as her reproach that I could stay alive for so many years, whereas she died a long time ago. Eighteen years, the age of majority.

I have already said that I had to reckon with the possibility of assumptions. Only later did a simple and logical conclusion occur to me regarding her surprise: she had left me as a twelve-year-old boy, and now she saw a thirty-year-old strapping fellow before her, her Albert, her Bertie.

But I alluded you can guess for yourself how, despite everything, our encounter was magnificent and enchanting. The initial surprise had completely vanished; we treated each other with such ease as if we had parted just half an hour earlier with the agreement to meet at this very same time and place.

The first thing I noticed about her was that she was not as talkative as she used to be. Her voice was still raspy and deep. But I noticed this too every word she spoke had its own weight, which I felt pressing on my heart, and she had to spice up each last word in the sentence with a smile, which seemed somewhat impenetrable to me and, at times, even icy.

I tried very hard to remain calm and hide this fact from her, but at one point she interrupted me... no, she interrupted herself to tell me that she knew very well what I thought about her somewhat impenetrable and, at times, even icy smile. This, of course, did not stem from her desire to show off in front of me, or to appear a little offended that everyone had written her off and pretty much forgot her, but because she felt confused in a world long not her own for so long, and if you want to know all, she could hardly wait to return from where she came.

- Do you have someone there? I blurted out.
- I have you there she replied.
- You have me here – I said.
- I never had you here she said. You can only have someone with whom you live in memory. Everything else is just a short-lived illusion and fog.

Personally, I was irritated by her heartlessness in saying that I wasn't there, and I was sitting right across from her.
- So, what am I to you then? – I almost shouted on the verge of tears.

She pulled both of her delicate hands from the table and then placed them on her lap, responding to my anger by saying that it was pure, one-hundred-percent idiocy that I could not understand some of the simplest things. "Besides" she said – "there's time for that too", but that I would truly belong to someone only when someone remembered me and not when someone was looking at me in front of them like she was looking at me that moment, or I at her. "It's completely different when you stand before someone, forcing them to acknowledge your presence and occupy their mind with your being. And this, again, is what a man thinks about a man: how to remove the other to have more space and more peace. To have more bread and air. But over there!? Over there, no one bothers anyone because there is no vanity."

- Not even nostalgia for life? I asked wistfully.
- There's no such thing she replied.
- Not even for me? I was taken aback.
- I am always with you she said calmly.
- Then why were you surprised when you saw me?
- Because I always keep you in my memory the way I saw you the last time, when I blew you a kiss through the air. In particular, I often recall the image of you holding a broken sugar rooster in your hand and being angry that it had no head, while sister Tereza comforted you, mildly scolding you that it wasn't nice of you to cry over a broken off rooster head when your mother was going to the hospital, after which you brutally hit her on the shin and screamed at the top of your voice that roosters also love life and don't want their heads chopped off. Do you remember how that time I was wearing this same blue muslin dress that I'm wearing now?

What could I say? I dared not think about anything because mother would already manage to guess out loud what I was thinking about. If I had thought about something nice related to her, she would surely have said that I wanted to ingratiate myself with her, which would, I believe, only deepen her disappointment in me since she had already told me that "over there", they are all completely devoid of vanity, and thus of the need for flattery. If, on the other hand, I had thought of something bad, she would understand that I wanted to leave her aside, which would later be my alibi to forget her, or rather, to rarely think of her.

Only then did I realize that her visit might very well be connected to the fact that I hardly ever thought of her. I must admit I didn't even think of her on the anniversary of her death. Yes, I think she showed up to remind me that it was not at all nice or fair of me, so, if necessary, she came to me to discuss whether something wasn't right between us or if it was a consequence of our breakneck speed of life, and thus the indifference towards everything passing us by.

- It's true that you didn't think of me today either she said.

The same smile appeared on her face, but it was neither somewhat impenetrable nor a little icy, rather a conciliatory one in which I felt some piquant cheerfulness owing to my evident fear of how skillfully she read my mind. The thoughts imposed themselves, and whatever I thought, it couldn't be pleasant for this encounter of ours after so many years. We both had to act like we were happy. This, apparently, encouraged her even more to reproach me, so she finally noticed herself with some boredom on her face: "I have become vain again, and I am ashamed of it. Do you reject and despise me?"

- I don't know, mom I replied vaguely.
- Forgive me if I hurt you.

I couldn't help but laugh, amazed and a little surprised at the way she said it. I remember she was always gentler towards me than towards Tereza, who was two years older than me and, on top of that, so stubborn that the whole household would lose their minds over her. Father and mother used to argue for a long time after that, and I would cry in the other room, which was darkened, squeezing with all my might the neck of the wooden horse to make me feel better, while Tereza, as if having achieved her goal only then, would be absolutely calm, reading a sci-fi comic about Flash Gordon under the light of a wall lamp. Such heartlessness! Because of her, I started biting my fingernails and wetting the bed at night. I felt sorry for my quarreling father and mother, but also glad because they now slept in separate rooms, so I knew they couldn't even theoretically do those things anymore.

Thus, I protected myself from the outside world with fantasies, but over time, without noticing, I also separated from it. By my side I had my mother, whom I adored, loved above all, and because of whom I suffered, my father whom I neither loved nor hated, and my sister whom I despised and spent years figuring out how to get back at her but never found the convenient way to do it.

Then I decided to stop before I completely spilled everything. I don't claim that I managed to fully convey everything I saw and experienced in the dream, but more or less everything was as I wrote.

IV

YOU THOUGHT WELL, OH ALBERT, SO BEHAVE LIKEWISE

For as long as I can remember, the thought of my own death has always both attracted and frightened me. I could never fully grasp that a man who had been struck by it really no longer existed because I constantly felt that he had temporarily taken refuge somewhere, gone for a certain period of time, that he would surely come back someday, even if that day we also happened to be somewhere else I think I never doubted that. In any case, I believed, oh my, how fiercely I believed, that we would meet somewhere but where?not even God himself could know, nor does it matter, but that it is the final parting with someone you saw walking, moving limbs, chewing with lips, burping, loudly breaking wind, shouting, threatening, stealing, running away, hiding, lying, doing those things, and indeed, sometimes even creating a new living being well, I could never wrap my head around that. Sometimes I would rage to the point of tears over this fact, asking myself, loud and clear, why things are arranged that way between life and death, between God and manon one side, and between the devil and manon the other side, and why exactly our species, which prides itself so much on its intelligence, is not spared the very same fate that inevitably befalls every plant and animal. Hunger, guts, feces...

I only understand the death of those I didn't get to know; it's the only logical one for me because they were dead to me while they were alive. The only difference is that, in the first case, I can never meet them again, while in the second case, the chance of meeting them was 1:1,000,000,000. Horrifying, to say the least.

It was of no use proving to myself in utmost excitement that everything I saw and felt was not true, but an illusion in the form of a dream ugly or nice depending on what impression or influence I was under at the time, and thus, I soothed myself and somehow managed to comfort myself at the drop of a hat, allowing my imagination to keep exploring, probing, searching, approving, and accepting the kind of life that surely awaits me and the one currently perceived by my senses. Admittedly, I don't usually marvel at other things, except as I said if it concerns death, and not so much because I am afraid of it, but because I cannot understand it, and therefore, I have no right to be amazed at anything ordinary that wouldn't stem from a normal desire to change certain states of my soul about which I will speak in more detail a bit later.

I do not belong to people who live for the sake of completing some of their works in the name of some greater idea so that it will mean something to someone. I must admit that I envied such individuals for their willpower and faith that their very idea could benefit someone. It takes guts to believe so idiotically in oneself. This idiotically must not in any case be taken literally in the sense of being feebleminded, but it's an allusion to firmly, to the end, unconditionally because devils strive from all sides to take away your strength, faith, and will.

I'm still not quite clear about the spiritual role these ideas might have. After all, it is clear to me that they exist, that there is some hidden intent, but whence comes this impetus to attach second-class importance to this mere vegetation of ours and to shift it to a subordinate place, thereby giving precedence to some imaginary, general idea? This, honestly, was never clear to me, nor will it ever be.

My sister Tereza usually sat on the divan with her idiot (now this is literal) son from her first and only marriage whenever it was time for my arrival. If I happened to be late coming home, neither of them would budge in the slightest from their pharaonic positions. They would continue sitting like two wax figures until I arrived, even if I were to show up in the morning. And as soon as I opened the apartment door, I already knew that my sister would say: "Ah, it's you!", and I would reply like a clown with the learned text: "Yes, Rezika, it's me!"

As soon as I stepped into the hallway, she would appear at my feet to place two rags under them, on which I would slide across the polished floor. It was a double benefit: not dirtying the floor while polishing it at the same time.

Only in the living room would I officially kiss Tereza on the forehead and caress her idiot Adrian, that is, my nephew who could not take his idiotic smile off of me, the smile that caused constant drooling and the saliva hanging from his chin like an icicle. I also had to caress his cheek and tell him what brand of chocolate I had bought him. At that, he would gnash his teeth with satisfaction, stand up so giant- like, spread his huge legs and shift from one foot to the other saying: "Beto bought Adian choco... Beto bought Adian choco... Giiiive!"

He would, without fail, roar in the end.

So, my life was quite monotonous, taking place between school and home where, again, every livelong day I would always be greeted with the same cold, metallic greeting from my sister Tereza and her idiot son from her first and only marriage, and every time at the door they would, without fail, push those two rags under my feet for a double benefit: not dirtying the floor while polishing it at the same time. My goodness, is there a man who doesn't wish to change the scenes of his daily life.

Tereza's greeting never lacked her well-known pharaonic smile; there was not as much of it as you would like, but it was present just long enough not to let her culture and worldly upbringing fail. My soul felt, while I was still climbing the stairs to the apartment, that under no circumstances could such a gesture of her attention be a sign of love, but, first of all, the most ordinary bargain or order, whatever, the kind that heartless and calculating people set on themselves.

It would be needless to say that my sister Tereza and I agreed on almost all principled matters, which certainly couldn't have been missed by a more attentive observer such as our housekeeper Eva Tvrdi. As can be inferred from her last name, Eva would most likely be Slovak by nationality, and as I found out later, personally from her, she came from the vicinity of Daruvar. Basically, not at all preoccupied or overburdened with superfluous worries, she sometimes managed, in a ludicrous and relaxed manner, to make us both laugh sincerely, and she always mischievously spiced up her jests with some dirty jokes, which normally could not be met with indifference by the two of us.

I'm not going to talk about my father Ferdo, or as he liked to coddle himself Ferdinand of Habsburg because that conceited and self-infatuated asshole's floating, lecherous smile never left his face, especially when a woman would be close to him, regardless of whether he was being pierced by my sister Tereza's X-ray eyes, or sitting before his mother, my grandma Anastasia, who was silently fingering the rosary beads.

I think Tereza noticed that Eva has intrigued me too much lately. Although nothing happened between us, which would be worth mentioning, whenever it got dark, Tereza always had something to do near me at that hour or, if she had nothing to do, she sat next to me with that ornament son of hers and asked me something, mostly incoherent, which made absolutely no sense, for example, the gnocchi were excellent today, Albert, weren't they, or even worse and more miserable, it must be drizzling in Northern Ireland now, I would dare bet you anything.

Yeah, Northern Ireland. If only she had chosen St. Thomas Island, I guess I would have felt better. What kind of schemes are these: the north is for snow and rain, and the boring, drizzly, mizzly one at that, the south is for sun, laughter and courtship. Well, Northern Ireland is drier than Yugoslavia.

Out of sheer agony, I had to smile at her efforts to keep me from getting involved with Eva. What else could one think of that simple-minded girl but that a hen would sooner reject a rooster than she would someone's wooing. And to make matters even worse and more thorough, it was all so true that I simply didn't even dare to show any exasperation, which she would most likely take amiss and interpret as my malice, and that would further reinforce her jealousy and even more strengthen the suspicion of my honorable intentions towards good-natured Eva, who, it seemed, was really unable to refuse a man.

All you men are the same Tereza used to say. Even if a woman had no head, no arms, no legs only a pussy you would go to bed with her. The only important dates in your life are when you get that thing up.

As I already mentioned, whenever I arrived home, Tereza and Adrian would inevitably be waiting for me, sitting on the divan. First, I would take the elevator up two floors, from where a few steps led to the mezzanine where stood a lacquered door bearing a screwed-on metal plate. From Eva's first day working for us, I immediately instructed her to always polish it with Sidol so that it would constantly shine and one could read from the stairs that Albert Wollensky, Professor, lived there. With certain pride, I would make sure to stop in front of the door, stand still for a while, listening to my own breath through the acoustics of the entryway. Sometimes I would take half a step back from the door, then return to ceremoniously place my shoes on the doormat, wiping my soles and pressing my right index finger against the doorbell button, waiting for Tereza's footsteps in the hallway and her voice saying: "I'll be right there". With my eyes closed, I could imagine how she would appear, gaudily adorned with various pieces of fake gold jewelry around her neck and on her hands, where the first signs of wrinkling could be seen, and for the millionth time, without fail, from her rouged, sensual lips, more African than European, the one and the same exclamation would flow, the script of which never changed: "Ah, it's you!", and I would instantly know or guess (even with my eyes closed) that under my feet were those two disgusting rags, which I was to use for double benefit: I wouldn't dirty the polished floor, and I would also polish it. Double benefit. The early bird catches two worms. Yeah, right.

I am a man who carefully hides his emotions from others. I even went so far as to consider myself seriously grieved and depressed if someone managed to sense them with a more open and indiscreet question, which I would view with so much mistrust that I simply would not be able to minimize it to the point of completely neglecting it as innocent, misguided curiosity, simply offhandedly and inadvertently uttered. I made efforts to be unapproachable to everyone, restrained and not too mysteriously shrouded; I wanted to leave the impression to those around me that I knew only what I needed, and not that I knew nothing at all, because it was clear to me from my experience that it would even more increase the suspiciousness, without, on the other hand, hurting my intimate feelings, which, again, on their part or so it seemed to me was to a great extent quite touching and humorous.

Without a doubt, I should start the story where, for the first time, I mention my memories, which put me in the unusual relationship with all those lines I previously, above presented and which, in fact, communicate that there indeed exists my sincere intention to save things from oblivion and thereby make them significant enough to be very easily an accusation against me, or irrelevant, which is more likely, so that they become so unimportant, even banal, and thus free me from any responsibility before myself. In either case, it would be my own weighing of passions, so to speak, at the last moment, and everything that somehow had almost completely evaporated from my mind or was about to evaporate.

When I clearly decided to "put things on paper", the decision initially seemed rash, especially when, in the first days, I spent hours staring at its whiteness and thinking: what interesting do I have to say about what has happened to me lately? Phew, big deal, similar things happen to everyone, and no one finds it appropriate to waste time on them. This tug of war with myself lasted until I brought to light a modern linguistic expression and style in my sentence, and then things took off on their own.

V

KILLER AIR. EVIL PASSIONS EXIST BECAUSE OF THE MIND. MAN IS MAN BECAUSE HE IS MAN

I liked to talk along these lines, especially in a humorous form on top of that smiling halfway while reflecting on past events with some surprise and astonishment, and since this almost always triggered the feeling within that I no longer belonged to this planet or "normal" humankind, I perceived it as pulling myself into the abyss, a rather unusual grotesque, and the quickest way that would inevitably lead me to a situation where I had to do something.

So, let me begin.

I am Albert Wollensky. My last name is spelled with a double-u, a double l, and the mandatory wye at the end. As I write this, I am smoking and smiling. Is it arrogance or idiocy? I don't know. I don't even know why I'm smiling; simply, it's just driven by some inner impulse. Irony is the only weapon of the helpless.

I try to evoke a sense of moral elevation within myself, but the thought I summon escapes me and becomes blurry, and I must admit this task seems fruitless to me and that therewith I am kind of making a buffoon out of myself. I still have respect and decency left, so I ask for forgiveness if repulsion towards what I am about to present seeps in, because it is undeniable to assume that I will generously, without doubt, beyond all measure, consider myself the main culprit if I fail to accomplish what I feel a strong need to do: to sit in front of a blank piece of paper and fill it with my genuine confidence.

As usual, I have constantly held some fear within me that I want to consciously suppress, to no longer be exposed to the temptation of declaring it some kind of complex or frustration, although there are certain indications for such claims. Naturally, this did not suit my own feelings, although I would most gladly replace all that horror I must hide from others. It often overwhelmed me when I simultaneously felt sweaty palms and armpits, and I would inevitably seek a way to free myself from the presence of the person near me at that moment, as my nerves would not allow me to doggedly keep on feigning patience and composure, and pretending to be a puppet or a mannequin. It was simply about not falling into some kind of recklessness, such as for example someone noticing my physical torment that I wrestled with and, as of lately, I've had a harder time containing, so I wasn't sure how it was going to play out the next time. This defense mechanism was meant to save me from many inconveniences and prevent the eruption of accumulated anger. Nothing could be predicted, although there were many warning signs.

At the time when the state of my health was worrisome and I felt as if someone strong was pinching me all over my body with two fingers, I then had a burning desire to write, to write an awful lot, to share my wretched torment with that indifferent friend-paper.

What for? I would often ask myself. Can a word written on paper comfort more than a word spoken within and only to oneself? This, of course, most often gave rise to a feeling of depression and rejection within me, when I remained powerless and vague over the unfinished or fruitless sentences that I most sincerely believed mocked my torment even more, and now, on top of that, I am being weighed down by my ineptness and probably a lie of appeasing within myself the demons and my angelic childlike face, the appearance of which made everyone fall for it without exception, thus everyone claimed and swore on their honor and reputation to my sister Tereza that I had to be a truly good man, and that my moments of agitation were surely a result of oversensitivity, which is the characteristic only saintly people have, who silently take on both their own and other people's torment. "Look at that smile of his, only a saint's halo is missing above his head."

With an unusual pinch of lucidity, I could very easily imagine the text as a whole that had yet to be written, but only while lying facing the wall and thinking, staring at its whiteness. Sentences sprouted out of me by themselves, just as I wanted to see them written on paper, and then, cautiously, like a tomcat sneaking up on its prey, I would slowly get up, trying to hold on to what I had established in my mind as looking good, even making an effort not to ruminate so that no thought would twist and go crazy, and thus fall into an order that I wouldn't want it to fall into and with which I would not be satisfied.

But as soon as I sat down, it seemed that by the time I unscrewed the pen cap over a thread, everything would suddenly vanish out of my mind; with some pathos and a sorrowful longing, I would haplessly scrawl on the paper and scribble down my "feelings" in some dead, stale words that left a bitter taste in my mouth and increasingly confused and hurt me, driving me to such sadness that I could easily cry my heart out at any moment. In the end, utterly broken, I would lay my pen on the crossed-out lines that no longer bore any resemblance to those sentences that, just a moment ago, sounded so beautiful to me while I was lying facing the wall and thinking about myself, staring at its whiteness. To complete the picture or make it more amusing, I would try to revive them by lying again in the same spot, turning towards the same wall, thinking about the same guy, and staring at the same whiteness; but now, neither the wall nor its whiteness provided any benefit. I was already quite far from what had driven me to sneak towards the blank paper.

Can I be sure that it was even worth anything? Man is constantly imagining and seeing things.

I must admit one more thing. If I fail to write what I feel, at least I know whether there's something worth mentioning. These are the reasons why I often write uncontrollably, irresistibly, abruptly, and swiftly, and then, after everything, I am suddenly overwhelmed by that so familiar feeling of depression when I no longer know if my insides are splitting from my soul; mostly, an immense and immeasurable sadness prevails over being alive at all, for anyone being alive at all, because life is a big joke on man, a nasty joke that it wouldn't in the least be such if man didn't take it so seriously. Then, the emptiness in which I float as if in a boat without oars, completely fed up with myself and the impressions around me, makes me want to cry, to cry out loud until my shoulders shake and until my whole-body trembles, and to wash away with tears all that torments and frantically clutches me from within and weighs down upon me. I am still the only conversation partner to myself who neither speaks, nor scolds, nor criticizes, nor praises, but stands or sits here, beside me, wanting to help me, but not knowing himself how to do it without hurting me in my fragile state. I feel he desperately wants to, or I attribute that passionate desire to him. his proximity comforts me, although I don't know if it can be of any use to me. Then I wish to write, and by writing the real one I would simply fall apart if I manage to fill myself with words. Then again, I wish to not exist at all, to not be among the living, and it seems to me that true happiness would be if I had never been born at all; my parents, Ferdinand Wollensky and Ursula Wollensky née Esch, would have done a wonderful miracle by not giving me life, sparing themselves the unnecessary trouble of raising me and at the same time freeing me from the constant feeling of shame and guilt for being alive due to someone's physical whim.

It is unnecessary for me to emphasize that I prefer to spend my life sleeping because such a life would not protect me either. I believe I would immediately deny my existence and remain helpless and completely alone. If that were to happen, no one could deny that my life was not somehow connected with comedy, and here I would add with a dark joke as well.

I have so much on my heart to say, so I consider it wisest to speak first about things without caution and without benefit to myself, although it would not be remiss to apply a certain tact so that the image of a weirdo and a maniac does not come to the forefront, even though I have never tried to deny this to myself but only to point out certain facts that created him, facts that would later vanish into thin air, without which I would indeed be reduced to an insensate wraith just lurking in the shadows. Excitement overwhelms me as I write about things etched in my memory, causing me now a somewhat painful wistfulness, and I admit it is a considerable effort for me to explain and present them as cold facts, not as a lawyer's distance plea. Will those listening to these bold words of mine be ready to understand me, to ensure that my words are not spoken in vain, and to take my truth with a certain tinge of reproach directed at the one who confesses it?

Good weather was less painful because then I could take out a sun lounger and stretch out in the sun in the garden in front of the house. The garden is miniature: a laurel hedge, an ornamental fruit tree, some asparagus, and a pine tree barely holding on.

Does this intimate picture contribute to an explanation acknowledging that nothing outside attracted me anymore and that no one instilled confidence in me anymore? It has already been eighteen years since mom died, which all this time must have evoked unbridled, wistful associations in me, first concerning her death, and second, because in the past month she had appeared more frequently in my dreams than in all the previous years. I am neither astute nor insightful to guess why she now comes to my dreams more often, but I could not help but believe that it might be also because I have been thinking a lot about her lately, wondering what she would have to say while I was intensely suffering and coping. This would both comfort and anger me because I felt an increasing obligation to consider what she would do if she were in my place, or what advice she would give me if she were alive and here beside me. The truth was, though, that I had long since stopped seriously believing in myself or in her judgement, or in anyone's opinion, which I had to restrain in great fear if I found that I truly could not do anything against it.

I was usually dressed in a flannel shirt with vertical stripes, and I always took particular care to fasten the topmost button so that my neck was not visible at all. I liked to cross my arms over my chest and feel the chain of my watch turning around my wrist. My pants always had to be the opposite color of my shirt; otherwise, it seemed to me, I would not be able to control my emotions.

I want to continue and admit that I often grabbed the pen and then soon threw it aside, muttering that I did not choose the right time to write, and that I had to think about some things before I set out to elaborate on them. This seemed like a convenient excuse to myself, which was both a way to close my eyes to my public visibility and an alibi that things had not yet "fallen into place as they should". God save me from illusions; only fools still hope. Let me be indifferent and not notice anything, or better yet, let nothing distress or scare me, but let me enjoy everything, admire everything, and be happy that I can walk, that my intestines digest well and therefore I have a good bowel movement, rather than having my brain register everything with suspicion and that wistful smile which acquaintances believe is an expression of sanctity, and which I claim is only possessed by total idiots.

Why doesn't my life unfold without any memories and recollections? Why must they surface so intensely and so often? And could anyone find it so interesting to waste time on my shabby bravery to admit all this? It's hardly a wonder to confess to paper! Isn't it the wisest thing not to know anything? What good is experience but to hurt you. What good is knowledge but to show you what a zero you are, because you cannot be anything else but to see that you are a zero, and that's a great joy for them. How can they bother themselves? How can they bother others except, of course, with their stupidity.

All that's left for me is to mock myself. But for how long? Forgive me if I fail to recognize or understand much while I descend with horror into my own hell with the intent to free myself from this too heavy a burden. My impression is that I have never really been present in my own life and everything that has happened to me exceeds my spiritual capabilities.

Forgive me if I poorly control myself; I will find a way to horrify myself and somehow continue what I started. I admit that my fear plays a significant role in this, but I will try, at least here, to confront it. I admit that I often envy its superiority and the fact that it still holds me in its claws, although I strive to be indifferent. I cannot seem to drive it away, after which life would return to the right and hard path, and I would also stop feeling overly disturbed by the fact that I am constantly obsessed with my fate, which hasn't bestowed anything nice upon me.

- How do you feel? I repeated my mother's question from the dream once more.
- Roughly like a wound-up clock in an infernal machine I finally answer her now.
- That's not good, son says mom without excitement, but somehow sullen, as I remembered her when I used to return in dirty clothes from playing. That's not even smart, Albert. For whose sake? Only when I stop being afraid of death will you be able to be indifferent, and only then will no one be able to do anything to you. After all, why fear something you know is inevitably going to come? The living are mostly to blame for making death into a myth. That can never weigh on the dead. Death is most often a birth and a victory, and those who see it as a defeat are wrong. To understand that, you need a lot of conscience and no fear for your lousy zhizn...

VI

ISN'T THE ONE WE FEAR IN OUR HEARTS CREEPING UP SLOWLY? I MEET HIM BUT I DON'T RECOGNIZE HIM, I TALK TO HIM BUT I DON'T KNOW HIS NAME, BECAUSE HE SPEAKS WITHOUT USING THE LANGUAGE

The time when I dreamed of my mother, no matter how inappropriate it may sound, was filled with shame for what I was experiencing there. To put it mildly, I was always scandalized because of both her and myself for reviving some images, which caused my cheeks to burn intensely and my heart to pound with excitement for a long time. What is worth noting was my lack of pride, so in reality I would stare blankly at a certain spot for a long time, hoping it would divert my attention elsewhere, instead of returning to the dream and trying to explain why I was dreaming of my mother in a brothel, chasing her down the corridors to stab her with a knife; just as I was about to strike, she jumped out of the window, and then, when I leaned over, totally crazed, to see a human stew or the mush of my mother on the asphalt below, I only saw alleys of various neatly cultivated flowers, neon signs of some pubs flashing on and off, and when I turned around, I was horrified to see a ball of thick snakes on the bed, slithering down its legs, coming towards me, hissing and darting their forked tongues. I had nowhere to escape except to jump through the window just as my mother had done a bit earlier – but then, from somewhere, a saving thought came to me like a providence that this was a dream after all, and not reality.

What if it isn't a dream, though? First you wait to fall asleep, and then you are gripped by a mad fear that you will not wake up.

The next moments are agonizing as I wait to see if those snakes will return or disappear into the numerous holes that I only now notice in the walls, but alas, not only do they return, they are even closer to me and there are more of them an entire army! They slither and writhe with their forked tongues towards me, I clearly see that hollow fang, ready to bite into my flesh at any moment, into my vein, and release its dose of venom that will start wandering through me until it suffocates me completely.

And, by God, they would have bitten (one, I think, was already getting ready to jump) if they hadn't heard someone's voice from those numerous holes ordering them in some strange animal language to return, presumably, to where they had come from, because they really did return immediately, obediently slithering back towards the bed from which they had all just lunged at me. I heard a noise behind me. I turned around and I saw my mother at the window.

It was in May 1981, I think it was the last day, perhaps the penultimate, but that's not important now. In front of my sister Tereza, I made up some event where poets should read their works, and all the proceeds from this voluntary happening would go towards building a Home for Retarded Children. She was extremely touched by such humanitarian action by the poets and in such a mood, she wanted to come with me as well, just to get out of those four walls where she lived with her dim-witted son Adrian, to whom life had given only two things: heavy purulent pimples and huge buttocks thanks to which he never needed a belt, no matter the size of his trousers.

I decided to travel alone. I couldn't exactly determine if I had achieved my supposed intention to get away from home a bit and rid myself of certain nightmares that had physically exhausted me.

Night fell while I was in a compartment, seated closer to the corridor, among a group of chatterboxes. Three women and four men. At first, I wanted to cover my face with the curtain, to somehow shield my eyes from the overly bright light, but it had absorbed so much tobacco smoke and other unpleasant odors that I soon had to remove it from my face, revealing my scowling expression to the same blabbermouths, who did not miss my failed attempt to somehow separate myself from them and their stupid conversations with the smelly curtain, so an ostensible lady sitting across from me, holding a fashion magazine and fanning herself from the heat, instantly had to point out that it was still too early to sleep, and besides, our Balkan trains (unlike the wealthier West) were very uncomfortable and unsuitable for any kind of rest. Their freight cars were more comfortable than our wannabe Schlafwagen).

I kept silent and watched that slit of her mouth, not sure why, thinking, God, does she have a pussy full of o.b. tampons or a wad of cotton or, if she has children, does she use their torn diapers as pads? I immediately dismissed this third possibility because I know young mothers don't want to flirt with anyone, especially not through some filthy, stinking curtain. There are already more convenient ways for that.

She kept talking to me with a smile on those frog-like lips, constantly stretching them like Kermit the Frog, revealing two teeth between which I thought I saw a yellow filling. Surprisingly, it seemed to me that the trip was becoming more bearable as she started addressing me directly, bringing to the fore my private reasons for traveling, where I was traveling and why I was traveling. I replied that I was going to a seminar in Zagreb. "Why?" Why?I repeated her not-so-discreet question... because! For the purpose of exchanging opinions on some new types of special steels that could bring huge savings to our economy...

- How long will it last? She took me by surprise.
- What? You mean the seminar?...I snapped out of my lie. Three days I blurted out.

Why does our man usually deal with the numbers three, seven, sixteen, a hundred, a thousand, a million? A billion is already excessive. I haven't eaten for three days, I've been working like a beast of burden for seven days, sixteen hours a day... I don't know, let's say, I read, write, sleep... I haven't seen you in a hundred years, there are a million of them (children), but hardly anyone dares to say a billion. There are a billion Chinese, but surprise, surprise, over a billion. Do you follow the demographics, man? That's why the billion should be left alone.

- Three days? She repeated after me, excitedly.
- Yes, exactly three days, not a day more and not a day less I don't even know why I replied.
- Wonderful! Lovely! I envy you! She said.
- Why wonderful and why lovely? Why do you envy me? I asked nonchalantly, fearing that someone in the compartment might be a metallurgist who could prove in two words that I knew as much about steel as King Arthur knew about television.
- It's wonderful that you are linked to travel she was wringing her hands, trying hard to prove to me how wonderful it was because I was linked to travel. Your life is filled with changes, you come into contact with people who are similar to you and think the same or similarly as you simply put, you have fun, you live, as they say, to the fullest... so... what else can I say... you live a full life, not just vegetating like most.

I managed to smile somehow. I tried to oppose her, more to feign my modesty, that it wasn't exactly the right life as she thought. Besides, who knows where the right life is and when it truly is right. For me, perhaps your life is the right one, for you, my life is the right one, for Peter, Paul's life is the right one, and so on... I can live your life and not be satisfied, you can live my life and not be satisfied, and if we both lived some other lives, and flowed down some "other stream," perhaps we would be satisfied, while those who live them are not satisfied, they are perhaps even desperate to vegetate so, but would be satisfied if they could live our lives, like you wished to live mine a moment ago. Nothing is certain, we don't know anything, even though we think we know everything and have absorbed all God's wisdom.

- Bravissimo! She clapped her little hands, which she nearly broke a moment ago. You are a true poet- philosopher. You stroll through metallurgy and poetry as if you were in your own backyard.
- Ah, what can you do I spread my hands like a priest and slapped my thighs. I instantly felt ashamed of such unnecessary pretense and even smiled, but it was an idiotic smile, like the one Francis of Assisi had while talking to birds. But, by God, I didn't have birds on a branch in front of me like he did, so he had some right to smile at them. My smile was rather cretinous because I had in front of me a crude coquette who cared about special steels as much as about last year's snow, except she felt wet down below because of the lousy steel, unless it was what I had previously assumed.

And then I heard someone droning in my right ear:
- I've read about these new types of special steel. I turned to get a better look at the eager talker. Brush- like hair, a fat sweaty neck full of white hairs. Constantly wiping sweat with a handkerchief. Just what I needed. Such types have always disgusted me. But I knew one thing: if I reacted indiscreetly, I believe that it would only arouse more suspicion among those present in the compartment about what I had just been bullshitting in front of this pussy. After all, what does it matter if they figure me out, they can just suck it. I'll tell him I'm not in the mood to talk about it and ask him to leave me alone. If this broad had already lured me out of hiding and "forced me to reveal who I am and what I am", that doesn't mean that you and others can pester me in that direction and expect press interviews or, rather, interrogation, right? Besides, she at least has that thing, and what do you have? That bull's neck, that hair with which you could scrub the floor, and a tuft of white hairs as in a Yorkshire pig.

God forgive me, without any hypocrisy, I don't know why I was so nasty then. I allowed myself to babble in front of those I previously held in contempt like turkeys. Why did I need such a lie? Wasn't it more honest to say: "Listen you all, it's none of your business where I travel, and please leave me alone!" That's what I should have said. "I don't care who you are. Fate intended for us to be fellow passengers on this train tonight, so let's do it so let's make the most of it humanely. People whine to each other on the night trains, confiding their dirty secrets to each other, and then go back again to those who dragged them into all this shit and had them meet random owls. Oh, God! Oh, God, do you see this?

To me, any of these seven fellow passengers could have just walked out of the bank with a bag full of stolen money. I think that's a problem for the police, not for my curiosity. Anyway, most money in the banks is dirty money: the owners will be of a similar ilk; the only difference is in the way to get it in the pockets where they will deposit it or in another bank. With some, the style is discreet, while with others it is indiscreet. Things should be done with charm, with the obligatory Anglo-Saxon smile, not showing your teeth and letting a curse slip out. God, what do the police do?

- Listen! I began cautiously and reservedly in an unspecified direction anyway. I felt my big toe curl in my shoe out of frustration with myself for being weak and compliant, so much so that my ankle started to hurt. Special steel I began to shake my head like a horse at the starting gate before a race. Um, how can I explain this simply and briefly without being tiresome or, as our folk would say boring. You know, there are so many interesting things for such a kind of conversation.
- Feel free to use your terminology, I will surely understand you – he said deadpan as if behind the counter glass at the Social Security Office.

What does this sentence mean? Feel free to use your terminology, I will surely understand you. Does it mean he might be some fucking metallurgist putting me to the test so as to mock me in front of these people, showing that my earlier statements had nothing to do with the truth and that I was caught in a lie; and the night is long, it's warm and comfortable here in the compartment, and all the other compartments are full, packed. This jerk wants to teach me a lesson in public morality and the culture of interpersonal relations. On the other hand, perhaps he's well-meaning, a dude who will make an effort to understand me, even if I fill his head with various professional terms in the sense that every day you should learn something useful, learn, learn, and only learn. If I had said that somewhere, no one would have noted it, but they would have probably sent me back to where I came from, screw it old man, tens of thousands are waiting for a job; who cares about my learning, I only starved and lost my nerves while reading those thick books.

Well, now I had to talk about the latest types of special steel. I couldn't just seduce this one with general conclusions about how they could be used for huge savings in our country's economy, the way I did with that chick across from me. I only know that steel is as hard as it gets and that it's brittle, so it can break, and that there is some kind of gray steel. And also: steel-blue is the color of the sky. I'm not sure if I should say there's also blue steel. So, it is better not to mention the blue steel, or he might realize I'm totally clueless. I know there are also those kinds of special people, special steels, special police, specialists for this and that who are boring and know nothing under the sun except how to annoy and pretend to be curious, but in fact, it is futile to look for bad and malicious intentions in their words. Boring, and that's it. I ordered myself to be extremely cautious and suspicious about any kind of statement regarding these damned steels. I agreed with myself, like a buddy, not to engage in arguments but to limit myself to agreeing: yes, yes, indeed, of course, in any case, I absolutely agree, of course, very much, without a doubt, everything is relative, I will respond: yes, yes, the theory of relativity, Einstein, mc^2. Why on earth did I need all this? *em* is mass, *cee* is the speed, and the *two* is squared: *em cee* squared.

Isn't it enough that I politely and decently said who I am and what I do (a specialist in special types of special steels), and why I said that when I am not that, instead of saying that I am a professor and a poet, is not at all clear to me at all. What is the difference between a poet and a metallurgist in terms of social treatment other than the fact of how much I, as a person engaged in language and literature, am burdened with it. Am I a man truly marked by some internal signs, because the persistence with which people don't give up on me tells me that no external signs give me away in front of them. What I communicate is inspired by the purest and softest words, usually seasoned with an oriental humble smile and cheerfulness, which make me draw myself in even more so that they accept me more intimately and come closer to me, instead of slightly repelling them with these very signs so that they get used to it with me as something completely normal.

I think it's mostly because of fear. Well, I don't need to be afraid before Tereza, so I don't need to speak purely and softly in front of her, or with a smile and cheerfulness. She only needs one of my words to sense its intonation and instantly know what I meant by it. Before others, I have to say a lot more and then explain afterward what I meant and what my ultimate intention was, and I still see that many things are not clear to people at all, but my smile, which I don't take off my face, reassures and comforts them that I can only be a good man, a truly kind soul. When I realized that this was so, I decided to always play that card.

So, let's get back to special types of steel.

- You see I nodded in a profound manner as a sign that I wasn't quite sure I could explain it to him simply. I don't know how it would have ended if the woman across from me, obviously annoyed by my new colleague, hadn't croaked: "Well, you're not going to talk about that nonsense again, are you? In that case, I'm going to the corridor, into the draft, so hats off to you, gentlemen!"

The remaining two women supported her with giggling laughter, while the curious one was angry and protested in front of the three men that he didn't, couldn't, and wouldn't allow anyone to tell him what to talk about; he too, until a moment ago, had to listen to stupid conversations about fashion, rags, and what not. Well, Well, money and money are wasted there, that's why we're in this mess now because we wanted to be modern, and we haven't even properly taken our *opanci* off yet, and God knows how much more he would have babbled if that same lady hadn't interrupted him with obvious nervousness in her voice: "Don't you see that you're completely alone in your opinion in quotation marks and I don't really know where you get such persistence, not to say stubbornness, to get the upper hand over us and to talk such a topic as special types of steel, for which I am sure you are a total layman. Totalissimus!

- What does it matter to you, yourself personally, with whom I talk and what I talk about with someone? Are you my wife? He asked, all flustered.
- Fortunately, I'm not she replied.
- Listen! I intervened let's now leave the steel for another time. If you are really that interested, you will give me your address, and I will send you all the material from the seminar about it, and no more worries, right? I think that in a way the mesdames, misses it doesn't even matter no ware right. Imagine, I have to talk about it tomorrow from ten to one in the afternoon. So, how to explain everything in three or four sentences without bothering those present, right?

Bravissimo! Clapped the lady again. You can immediately see who is an intellectual; knowledge + upbringing + modesty + chivalry.

I dare say that she was at least momentarily in love, even though I made no effort to give her a reason for such feelings. Life, at times, played tricks on me, although I was glad to realize that I didn't mind it being so. Look, Albert I told myself evil can quickly turn into good, especially if you don't let it lead you on its leash for too long. You see, you must take an opposite stance towards your bad mood and find the strength to laugh when you want to cry and cry when you want to laugh, not just cry when you want to cry and laugh when you want to laugh. It can be both amusing and disgusting, and the man will continue to be considered as unfortunate because he doesn't even understand himself anymore, except he has some small justification for himself, which is in fact self-forgiveness.

The face of my fellow passenger across from me was glowing, and her eyes were shiny as if they were floating in oil. I understood her state. It cannot be denied that there was a certain and vague desire for adventure that freed her somewhat from initial reservations. I was also glad that I didn't have to play the melancholic in front of her. I won't deny that I felt somewhat exalted, even though my position and my hidden anticipation made me uneasy. Much as I showed some signs of affection towards her, though only as much as I could restrain from an unbridled urge within me, I couldn't help but realize that the calmness of my soul wouldn't be bad either, as well as the desire to curb some of my passions, which seemed to have flared up during our conversation dominated by her ringing alto seasoned with laughter, which she could not control at all, so every now and then she had to cover her frog-like mouth with her palm thus hiding that yellow filling and, by God, a gap on the side where a tooth was missing.

It was clear that she was increasingly unable to control herself, that our conversation was a real trial for her, that she was blindly infatuated with herself and what had led her there, and that it all merged into her personal resistance to own temperament it seemed to me the same thing that happened to me, so to speak, a sudden, more sublime life in harmony imposed itself and presented itself to us as a logical consequence of our dissatisfaction at home. Although in the course of our conversation empty gestures prevailed, both mine and hers, and the clowning that would have been prosaic and boring to us as husband and wife, even disgusting, just freed us from unnecessary considerations and from what we were hiding too much within ourselves. I felt a frantic strength inside me and thought that man really needed just a little to be at least a bit happy, just enough to recover from the torment filling his everyday life.

Why should you submit to everyday fate, although the malicious ones could rightfully claim that this is also fate to meet a young, beautiful lady in a night train compartment while bearing within a painful thought about last night's dream about your mother, and she the one across from you breaks it like a soap bubble just because she thinks you are someone important since you are traveling to a seminar where equally smart and wise people, together with you, will discuss the latest types of special steels and think about the ways to bring great savings to the state.

What is she bearing when she's grinning like this with an unknown man? Perhaps an even greater torment than he has: a painful conversation with her husband, if she even has one? Who is this young woman and where is she traveling? I didn't use my law-of-reciprocity right to ask her that. What does she want, or if I use the conditional what would she want? I overlooked many things while chatting with her, and even now, while pondering this. The silly grimace remained on my face and my eyes rested on her as a sign that I was keenly following what was coming out of her frog-like mouth.

Can one achieve a sublime life with lies? Is man, perhaps, God's illusion?

I never doubted that I loved Arabella, my fiancée from my youth. The only thing I wasn't clear about was whether my love for her stemmed from decency, pity, or a desire to be correct, which year by year made my position before her more difficult and, consequently, our mutual feelings. Thus, over time, we became two dignified and funny puppets whose only problem was whether to serve the spoons first and then the forks, or both at the same time, or whether to wipe ourselves with paper or cloth napkins, the latter needing immediate washing after use while the former could be easily thrown away and weren't nearly as expensive as the detergent needed to wash the latter.

This is how Arabella spoke in her gentle voice, which made me strain my ears to understand that Eva hadn't salted the fish soup enough. Besides, I never managed to see that clitoris in Arabella's throat in the two years we were together, and I already spotted it once in this croaker sitting across from me.

The young lady across from me lightly touched my knee with her finger, repeating a question I had overheard, and I concluded she was asking me something by her questioning facial expression, accompanied by that artificial smile of hers, making me feel ashamed as it became evident that I hadn't been listening to her, having been lost in memories of Arabella.

- You were thinking about something? The lady preempted me.
- Yes I replied. I re0membered something for a moment. Sorry!

Of course, I should have said: I was thinking about my ex-fiancée, comparing the two of you. Why did I think of her at the moment I was just across from you? I don't know how to answer. Or perhaps: last night I dreamt of my mother in an indecent and inappropriate role!

How to tell her that, when the question would immediately follow of the equally indecent and intimate intensity with which I prompted them? They would have been right to be asked so, and I couldn't hold it against them.

It seemed she had a certain inkling of what I had to tell her and would have likely told her let's say had we been alone in this same compartment by chance. Night, train, woman, alone. Pathetic and disgusting. It wasn't that what I felt towards her was disgusting, but the external decor was, the one that often drives us to extract the best in us and poison it. Music, alcohol, drugs, loneliness, the sea, night... man is truly wretched and pitiful. God has every right to regret having created him in the first place. And then I loudly said:

And the Lord saw how great the wickedness of the human race had become on the earth, and that every inclination of the thoughts of the human heart was only evil all the time.

The Lord regretted that he had made human beings on the earth, and his heart was deeply troubled. So, the Lord said: I will wipe from the face of the earth the human race I have created, and with them the animals, the birds and the creatures that move along the ground, for I regret that I have made them.

My suspicion and caution had completely vanished. This provoked her reticence and precaution that she had been too talkative, so, as soon as she fell silent, I guess she only then noticed how her voice had filled everything before, because in the ensuing silence, the monotonous clattering of the coach wheels and their rumbling at the rail junctions were all we heard.

It wasn't the first time I had dug something out of another person, her look was telling me.

I searched for and gathered the strength to apologize for my absent-mindedness and distraction from her story, which she had already become a witness to. Despite this, I maintained that silly grimace and my wandering eyes on her, which thinking back resembled anything but a man genuinely following what was being said; thus, the cretinous gaze continued to wander over her, instead of doing something completely different.

Out of the corner of my eye, I noticed the outlines of our heads in the window glass, and then I saw that *he* was looking at me from there and mocking my confusion. I decided then to get off at the first station and wait for the first train to take me back home.

I conveyed this to her immediately, and she asked me right away: "Aren't you traveling to a seminar where the latest types of special steel will be discussed, which will bring great savings to our economy?"

The latest types of special steel. Are there old types of special steel or the oldest types of special steel? Head of Steel. Steely health. Steeling oneself. A will of steel. How the steel was tempered. "Čelik" (Steel) from Zenica defeated FAP from Priboj. During the match, a fight broke out among the players, but to the mutual satisfaction of everyone, the match ended in a correct and friendly tone. A cordial one!!

If there is grey steel, there is also grey matter in the brain. Its quantity affects a person's behavior, that is, whether they will fight in a given situation, at a given moment, and in a given place, whether they will be a friend, or even cordial. With cordial greetings, yours...

I stood up and straightened, holding my left leg in the air. Then I picked up my luggage and waited for others to move their legs so I could pass into the corridor.

- I remembered, actually, I forgot to tell you that I first have to get off at this place to visit a friend, just to see him, and then I will continue my journey on the first train in the morning.

- But you have a presentation at ten she insisted.
- In that case, I will have to find a taxi to get me to the seminar on time I replied in an English manner. All I was missing was a pipe and of course the English language.

I wondered why I felt the need to lie in front of her and justify my quite unreasonable action. However, I interpreted it by the fact that there was no voluntary poetic happening for the construction of the Home for Retarded Children, for the sake of which I had deceived my dear Tereza. She and her feeble-minded son Adrian would probably be waiting for me sitting on their divan. The fact that this lovely lady was part of the combination tonight was more of a random coincidence than a real need to justify myself before her. This thought led me to suddenly end the liking I felt for my new acquaintance, out of decency towards both Tereza and Arabella, which despite everything caused me a lot of trouble, effort, sorrow, and fear, but also filled me with pride in myself. Where did I get such a will to first bluff and then, like a child, scatter the neatly arranged toys and provoke anger? Yes, I saw it clearly, I clearly saw it on her face, because women's faces always reflect a simple affection.

We stood right next to each other face to face and looked at each other for a moment or two. My sadness and melancholy were evident as I had to lie to her, and in her eyes, there was an emptiness that I couldn't compare to anything else, perhaps the emptiness we feel when we rarely engage in something unpleasant, and even then, being let down. I believe she felt a painful pressure in her soul, so she couldn't hide from me the familiar way she let me know how much it troubled her.

She sat on the chair, and I remained standing in the same spot, looking down at her. The man who wanted to talk with me about steel was looking out the window into the darkness and boorishly muttered to himself, loud enough and vague enough for others to hear: "Whoa, dude! Yes, yes, he will!"

I disregarded it; I just noticed his boorishness. I continued to look in her direction. I searched her fingers for any sign that would tell me who this woman might have. I didn't notice anything except that they were beautiful, long, slim, bony, with well-manicured nails coated with clear nail polish. I felt pain while looking at her, and I was overwhelmed with immense shame as I looked down at her hair-parting in the middle, where the white strip of skin stood out, and I morbidly imagined that this same skull, without the skin, would lie in the ground, bare; and then I forced myself to start thinking in that direction, shifted all my weight to the right side, took the bag from the baggage rack, and stepped into the corridor.

- I knew it, miss, that he was a good-for-nothing, a swindler. The trains are full of them, and our police are always asleep I imitated in my mind the steel enthusiast who had been looking out the window into the darkness to see the grass growing in the meadows at night. Whoa, dude! Yes, yes, he will! I know such people, I travel often. It's enough for me to take a look at them and everything is clear to me. I can smell them.

That man would probably seek a psychology department if he read about my case in the newspapers. I don't believe he could recognize me because he was turned away from me the whole time, looking into the darkness. If he observed me in the window glass, it's not the same as seeing someone in a mirror, let alone face to face. It's not the same to say: Whoa, dude! and Yes, yes, he will! with one's head turned to the darkness and say the same thing grinning directly in your face. Who could take away your right to slap him immediately, and six witnesses would confirm that you were provoked? This way: Whoa, dude! and Yes, yes, he will! He could have said it to anyone in the dark, maybe someone was passing by at four o'clock after midnight, maybe someone was beating someone in the meadow, maybe someone killed someone, or maybe a star fell from the sky. I call the star dude, and what do you care that I call the star dude?

There you go!

I didn't dare to look back into the compartment for a long time, because I was haunted by the unpleasant feeling that her eyes were constantly watching me, and along with them, the eyes of those other idlers.

When I saw the lights of a settlement and assumed we would soon stop at a station, I glanced into the compartment as if by chance and was simply stunned and saddened by what my eyes registered. She was sleeping, and on top of that her hand was touching the hand of that oaf who had already managed to move into my seat. The strap on his wrist was about to burst, even though he had it on the last hole. Soon, the train came to a stop.

When I jumped off the high coach step onto my right foot, a different thought arose in me, confusing me, so I turned to face the train and saw only two letters on it: JŽ. I tried once more to picture what I had last seen, but her laughter, her alto, and the clattering of the coach wheels on the rails wouldn't let me. I thought: what if she was pretending to sleep, deliberately closing her eyes? What should I have done? I should have listened to the lust within me; anyway, in the worst case, my end would have been better than this, because now I have to listen to the lonely barking of dogs and the muezzin's call for the Asr prayer from the mosque minaret.

In the dark, I couldn't make out the letters on the station building. What place could this be? Once more, I saw the red light of the lantern on the last coach of my train, now disappearing behind the first bend. My attention was drawn to the two young men competing at this late hour to see who could walk longer on the rails. Then, suddenly, I heard footsteps behind me. With a flashlight aimed directly at my eyes, I saw someone approaching. Only when he got within a step or two did I see that it was a policeman.

VII

IT IS BECAUSE WE AND OUR LOVE ARE NOT ALONE IN THE WORLD. HERE IS ANOTHER ONE GOING THE SAME WAY, HIS FACE SMEARED WITH MUD AND HIS HEAD SPRINKLED WITH ASH

It only takes five minutes with my father to see, without being particularly perceptive or intelligent, that his ornateness and mocking tone were somehow always at the forefront, perhaps because of his blond hair and terribly red face, which I believed was due to his poor metabolism. "Shit sticks to him" I used to say maliciously. Later, I regretted such terminology and preferred to say that feces wouldn't leave him. Had I loved and respected him, I would probably have claimed that dad had a high blood pressure. Instead, we concluded it wasn't the high blood pressure but the other thing. I tried several times to bring this up, of course, when he was in a somewhat better mood, but either he didn't understand me and didn't insist on my conclusion, or he consciously ignored me to show, I guess, that he didn't at all take me seriously or consider what I said worth thinking about. Things between us simply stood in such a way that neither of us, most of the time, wanted to interfere in each other's lives, and therefore, we got used to living next to each other. We arranged the space between us so as to avoid the possibility of any verbal interaction, and the few sentences we would devise and force out of our mouths (if we exchanged them at all!) revolved around whether we needed to buy bread that day, how much milk should be bought, and who would buy it, or whether a household appliance was broken and should the service be informed about it.

With fear and concern, I was careful not to give him any reason to hurt me with those two horrible traits of his, and I worked hard to not be hurt with those two horrible traits of his, and I tried hard to keep them from reaching me, of course, as long as I didn't give a valid reason for that. It goes without saying that, in the first place, I wanted to avoid unpleasant memories of the past, above all my childhood, where I still clearly see the sad fate of my sister Tereza, whom he, at the very least, considered his private property to use whenever and however he wished. The matter was so painful that even then I seriously thought of killing him and thereby ending my childhood suffering. Then, to my astonishment, I realized that certain things cannot be done at a certain time, no matter how painfully they affect the psyche. I had to admit to myself that I didn't understand a thing, not a single thing. I said this then, though I still think that, out of fear of the consequences, I sought an alibi for myself to avoid doing what my heart dangerously yearned and strived for.

From afar, I liked watching that domestic despot torment my mother, enjoying it when he found some unflattering comparison for her or some trait of hers that I often considered a virtue. He would call her "chicken- brained", "bug-eyed like an owl", "what big udders you have" referring to her breasts, and similar insults. He called my sister "four-eyes" as he "found" a convenient word to consider her his four eyes, or he would refer to me before my mother something I heard countless times as Vito Genovese. By the way, on other occasions I was "that garbage" or "nobody and nothing".

There's no need to say that from then on, our relations became so cold and tense that I hardly even noticed them as such. Only his occasional attention would be so suspicious to me that I would feel more uncomfortable and uneasy from sheer distrust than when he behaved in his usual manner. Those rare moments of his good mood were often filled with unrestrained laughter, which was also hoarse, so whenever things were difficult and unbearable for me, I imagined him cold and wax-white in the grave, silent and decaying under the onslaught of worms.

Mother was a different story. Her, on the other hand, I constantly heard talking, talking, talking, always indulging in complaints, criticism, and advice to be cautious and to not get bogged down like she had gotten bogged down. She even took the liberty to advise us that marriage was the greatest stupidity among all the stupid things that man had invented. Her motto was: Marriage is ravage!

There wouldn't be anything shameful about this if she hadn't fundamentally changed the moment she would hear father open the door. I noticed this with some melancholy even as a kid, and I started to ponder what kind of relationship existed between my father Ferdinand and my mother Ursula. Why weren't they named differently? If I met any Ferdinand in the world, I would consider him an idiot, a beast that should be shot like an ordinary mongrel. If I met any Ursula in the world, I would sense sadness and wistfulness in her, the sorrow of a woman who had surrendered herself to a maniac and a tyrant.

Who could understand that?

Of course, I had to take into account her certain fear of him, because he often reproached and reminded her of his pistol from the last war, for which no one could ever determine with certainty where it was, or if it even existed.

I also think that mother used to bluff us quite a bit, bad-mouthing father in front of us while flattering him, in the belief that it must have pleased him and that she was doing it just to make him happy.

There was no question of any jealousy between them. Those few objections, when one stayed a little longer, were more a sign of grumpiness that such lateness was getting on one's nerves, something akin to giving one a crooked nail instead of the straight one. There was some secret bond between them; otherwise, how could it be that neither in my childhood nor in my youth did I ever see my mother cry because of him, except when she was furious and out of herself, openly thundering and cursing, sincerely beating her chest that this time everything was really over, and this time divorce was inevitable. She swore by God and the heavens, and the Bible, and her happiness, and the two of us who were all she had in this world. She would take me, and that bear, that bloodsucker, could take Tereza. Through the open bedroom door, I saw the wings of the wardrobe spread wide. From there came her forced singing "You only love once, everything else is an illusion", and her and her terribly poor pitch made Tereza and me stifle our laughter in the kitchen to avoid bursting out and dying from it. The first song was already half cut off, and mother sang that all her "autumns are sad" and, probably not knowing the rest of the lyrics, continued with la-la-la and lively flirted with herself in the mirror in some of her old dresses. I think that day she could have written dozens of letters to friends across the country, solemnly announcing that she would soon separate from Ferdinand Wollen sky, that she would take me with her, and that father would take little Tereza. That's how God wanted it, and she had nothing to complain about or hold a grudge against anyone, and she thought that in the same way, nothing bad could be attributed to her.

    I was becoming so uncomfortable with the gaudy colors of her dresses, her countless suitcases, her God knows where from creams, colognes, powders, lipsticks a full arsenal that I seriously considered closing the door of the bedroom, then of the hallway, then of the kitchen, to run to the staircase and close the front door behind me, door to door, all the doors in the world, so I wouldn't hear her going nuts upstairs because I knew that in the end, when she tired herself out from the passion, she would throw herself face down on the marital bed and only then let off steam by cursing her mother for giving birth to so-unfortunate her.

    I didn't notice one more, very important thing then: there was still a lot of time until three o'clock when father would come home; enough for the show to end on time all those numerous dresses would be put back in the wardrobe, and all and all those written letters would be carefully torn up and then burned.

    You see, Albi, we cannot change the circumstances!

Whenever such scenes happened, I would bet on myself that on that day, mother and father would be alone in their room for a long time, I would hear strange rustling sounds from there, like "hoo" and occasional growling mixed with giggling. Tereza and I would be sitting on the couch, embraced and somewhat confused. I would kiss her on the cheek, and she wouldn't return it, but she would offer it, wet with tears, until we heard the key turning in the door, and only then would we separate from each other.

Mother would come out first, smiling as if coming back from a journey, with the carrier behind her full of gifts for the children. That fop, scoffer and madman wasn't smiling, but he wasn't frowning as usual either, but was somehow solemnly hypocritical. He was approaching me with outstretched hands to shake my hand like a partisan: "How do you do? How is school? Do you have any Ds?"

I was already aware enough to not fall into the trap in which, most often in anger, struggled when he would take me for a ride like this. But I didn't want to spoil the mood either and give him an instant nerdy reply that everything was in perfect order. The conversation between the two of us lasted only a moment. For the sake of formality, he would usually end it by adding: "If you *neez somesing*, just ask. He who asks doesn't lose his way!"

And that's all.

Only mother knew how I felt, so I knew how hard it was for her.

I noticed my father making superhuman efforts to smile at me. I think he hated me even then because he had to pretend in front of me, all because of my mother, who had either just satisfied him or, on the other hand, threatened him with scandal, bleach, razors and all other suicidal props that could stand in the way of his career, which his superiors would certainly never want to forgive him, although they considered him promising and highly disciplined, and as such held him in highest regard.

That day, we would go on a mandatory outing by car to the outskirts of the city. No one could have guessed how my sister Tereza and I felt, and with us, indeed, my mother, who kept winking with happiness at us from behind my father's back, as if to say: "We got him this time. Just listen to me and leave the matter to me."

I wasn't surprised when sister Tereza once told me privately: "You know, Albert, I've lost all hope that mother will ever carry out her threats."

- That's good I replied.
- It's awful how she makes such a spectacle of herself. It's disgusting she said, but almost completely losing her voice at the end.
- What's disgusting, Tereza? I insisted.
- The way she shamelessly torments everyone around her. I'm disgusted with myself for having her blood in my veins.

There was indeed something nauseating and slimy about how that despot, out of fear for himself, coddled my mother with a subdued and rehearsed voice, so she often couldn't even hear what he was whispering to her, even though she had sharp hearing. And at night, the two of us huddled in front of their bedroom door in our fustian nightgowns, listening to them copulate out of interest, and then we'd hear him get off her and say, full of himself: "This *vaz* a terrific *fuk*!"

From the accent and the way he said it, I felt that he never put a question mark at the end of the sentence to verify, to ask if she shared such a conclusion; no! Quite simply, not one but three exclamation marks could easily be put without much exaggeration on his modest manhood.

- *Didya* see? He strutted, all puffed up and smug.

In short, I now admit a painful doubt in myself that I too had the honor of enduring all this without having the guts to at least leave the house. If I had, things would have looked completely different within me, and I wouldn't be ashamed of it. I would consider it an unfortunate fate, but as it was, I could add fear to it. I sought justification in the fact that I was not overly strict or thorough when it came to certain higher principles. One can experience distasteful and unpleasant things, but I knew there was a suitable way to bypass them. I admit that I always offered some vague excuses for that, postponing the exit for a near future, thus constantly stifling myself to avoid facing myself and giving up certain comforts that my father's home provided. I think the real truth lies in the observation that I was always afraid of my own shadow and my dream.

I am glad to find myself in the same position as him, knowing neither of us will move, even though we both know very well that we do not love or respect each other, and more so, that we cannot be indifferent to one another. For now, I was the only one in the family who included a part of the truth in what he said, although it became clear to me later that this was their conscious tolerance. Within me, sudden short- lived excitements and long depression lived side by side. Sometimes the two would somehow manage to blend so that I often had the impression that both of them were joking and making fun of me, ridiculing me, which always reminded me of something demonic that rages within a man, representing his comical struggle to cope with it.

I realized this one August afternoon while I was swinging on a swing strung up between two poplar trees in the garden, which must have been a perfect surprise for me. I should mention that I then congratulated myself on this comment, which was made without any sense of ambitiousness, without misery over despair, and surprisingly it did not make me sad or worried at all. I have always been, especially lately, a good and grateful audience for myself, capable of hearing both applause and whistles instantly, because I knew how to look at myself not with my own eyes but with hers, with her soul, which could be merciless, indifferent, but also enchanting and magnificent. When I mocked her, she didn't take it as a personal insult or become sad because of it. No! But even when I praised her, she accepted it with considerable reserve, always seeking the reasons for and the purpose of that praise. But, without any joke, there was always a game conceived between us to expose to ridicule either the devil or the angel, and to establish some sort of alliance between them. To my audience, I would speak about, let's call them smarter things for example the need for man's initiative to take his fate into his own hands, which often implied a certain harshness of feelings and ruthlessness of the soul.

In the event that this deal ceased to be valid, I wouldn't feel animosity towards her as long as she showed understanding towards me; after all, I laughed from the bottom of my heart since only then did she allow me to observe her closely.

Without any doubt, the two of us were an inseparable pair, friends-companions, needing each other, although, not so infrequently, we ferociously tormented each other like cat and dog I did it to conquer her, and she to test and challenge meso one day, this time not in August, I rightfully exclaimed in a fit of ecstasy: "I am a comical theater!"

It seems almost incredible that I could thus maintain some balance between myself and her. I feared she might deny me her visit just when I wanted the performance to begin. It made no sense for me to doubt it, because my audience was growing larger the lonelier I became, and I managed to ascertain, with undisguised admiration, that she increasingly admired me every day the more I mocked her, that is, that she increasingly mocked me the more I sank into despair.

It's hard to imagine a game more enjoyable to me than this one.

I could simply see that she was pleasant for me, primarily because I could no longer stand anyone and I preferred to enjoy the peace and quiet of a darkened room, stretched out on the chair. Father continued coming to tend to the plants, since Tereza had made it clear to both of us that the plants could not count on her care, because she had someone to worry about, she had Adrian and that said it all. She had an outlet for spending her energy.

Father would come with Uncle Martin, and the two of them took turns mowing the grass in front of the house, so that, in the beginning, I had to listen all day to the lawnmower and the snipping sound of pruning shears. The only comforting thought was that it would be done, the sooner the better, because afterward, I could stretch out peacefully on my sun lounger and watch the surrounding fields and the horizon where the chapel of the former church, now a resort, was clearly visible.

Those two poplars still disturbed me, although they provided shade and I usually tied my swing to them, but the loud noise in the leaves, which had over time become my obsession, disturbed me; those leaves rustled mostly just to disturb me, and sometimes it seemed to me that even without wind, they would flicker only to anger and provoke me.

Noise, noise... noise everywhere. Searing heat, wind. Searing heat everywhere, wind, wind everywhere. Where does all this wind, noise, and... children come from?...

VIII

NOT YOU, BUT MYSELF I PUNISH. AND WHAT IF SUDDENLY SOMEONE WAKES ME UP AND SAYS TO ME: "BE A MAN BEFORE YOU TURN INTO ASHES!"

I must say the following: no matter how friendly I tried to be towards children, or rather, tried to understand their need for running and playing, I began to feel resistance towards their unbearable clamor, which provoked a real outburst of rage in me, which in the beginning, I tried with all my might to hide by first putting my hands over my ears, and then, when that didn't do any good either, I plugged my ears with cotton wool, bandages, and put on Walkman headphones with Bach's music, but as it flowed in a slow and drawn-out rhythm, I replaced Bach with Vivaldi, but this time Vivaldi irritated me more than the children. It seemed that I no longer cared for any sound, tone, or voice, but only peace and rest in which I could enjoy and dream. The children's noise dissolved and dispersed my dream like the sun disperses fog, awakening and hurting all my overstimulated senses.

It's likely that they didn't do it with the malicious intent to spite me and cause me pain. The way they performed these antics left me cold and indifferent, even somewhat imbued with derision for my colleagues who stayed at school to continue working with children. I half pretended to not even notice them, as if their shouting didn't reach my brain. I even used to watch them through the window, and once, I helped a hidden boy find a safer hiding place, so the one who was looking for him started to cry, thinking he was left alone and that his friend was no longer alive. In the end, to each I poured a full glass of blackberry juice, which my aunt had sent by Uncle Martin.

I will never understand the devotion with which they accepted the glasses, and then, a moment later, as if seeking my permission once more, and after I nodded with a smile, they gulped them down. Then I approached both boys and asked them their names. One said his name was Marin, and the other said his name was Marko. For more than half an hour, I inquired about their studies, who taught them, and then, at parting, I poured each another full glass of blackberry juice, to which they both thanked me in unison and left with multiple farewells.

I am not a strong man. I am a man of medium height, once a true strapping lad from the waist up, as can be clearly seen in an old yellowed photograph taken in Kaštel Sućurac in 1971, on one of the many piers where I was standing with the hair growing from my skull like thistle, wearing a shirt buttoned all the way to the top button, with five-pointed metal buttons, looking serious and patient, as if the photographer, at the very least, was aiming at me and thinking of shooting me at any moment.

One sleeve was slightly rolled up so that the detail of how I wore a *Ruhla* watch on my left wrist could be recorded in history. Back then, I was more naive than good, thinking that jokes could drive away or at least bring the bureaucracy and nationalism to reason. I was so withdrawn into myself that I couldn't immediately understand the joy of everyone at home when father and mother excitedly announced that a letter had arrived from the Central Committee, which admitted to father that he had been wronged, that his appeal was favorably resolved, and that the culprits would be "adequately and statutorily punished".

*And all of zem, efry singl van!*father raised his finger in the air, beaming with some vengeful happiness.*I vill not schtop 'til I see zem all in prisson.*

I don't think even Cato Maior had raised his finger in such a way when he incited the Romans to Carthage.
- Ceterum censeo omnes hostes dellendam esse! I blurted out.
- *Vat are you blabbink, Alpert?* he came down on me.
- Nothing, I say it's good that they destroyed Carthage.
- *Don't let me karthago you up, you doggo. I vould see you if you ver in my situation. Damn you in my situation. Damn you ven you don't know zat now I vas born again.*

Mother, it seemed, was the happiest, she probably thought that no ugly words would be heard in the house for a while. Before anything else, she thanked God for the help: "First of all, dear God, thank You!"

All in all, there was something about it that quite reminded me of a farce and I dare say even disgust, because I believe it is inappropriate to shout at manipulators if you haven't taken the time to shout at yourself first. Later I remember I used to point this out to him with a malicious smile that had a touch of teasing, but he, it seemed, despite everything, did not care the least about my stings. It was far easier for him than for me because everything was simplified for him: things were either black or white. If there were any nuances in between, they escaped his simplistic way of thinking and concluding. Simply put, he was unskilled in finer and more nuanced thinking.

Until his death, he despised mansions, soft pillows, and civilized life. He liked to sleep in his suit, on an ottoman, without anything else. Whenever he saw me with a book in my hand, any book (he called all books "novels"), he would immediately slap me twice. Always twice. Once on each side. He only believed in weapons, orders, and punishments. His eyes were set on the past, and he loathed and detested anything new. If, by any chance, something new was brought up, and only if he was well-fed and well-slept, and a comparison was made between the old and the new, in such cases he was less inclined to use polite expressions and would badly curse and fortify his atheism with gods, which must have disgusted mother and offended her most intimate feelings. At that time, this was popular and, I guess, a sign that one belonged to the new era.

This was how my father thought and behaved. He had the true lumpenproletariat soul, because the inheritance his father had left him was not particularly large. It consisted of a small house, a ground-level one with a packed dirt floor, a half-starved little horse, and a stepmother who, apart from gold hoops in her ears and one silver-capped tooth in her mouth, had nothing left of her once-renowned beauty. She sat all day in a corner, sipping stale water and complaining about the heat. Sometimes she would feed crumbs to the sparrows under the window, and then she would suddenly wave her hand at them. The birds would instantly scatter to the nearby linden trees, and she would shout after them in a hoarse voice: "It's raining! Toot-toot!"

Her mouth was a bitter gash, cold and evil like a lizard's, dry, cracked, and jaggeda true pink fissure.

In that photograph mentioned earlier, I said that I was a strapping lad from the waist up. From the waist down, one could clearly see my left foot in a high orthopedic shoe with a raised double sole, and between the metal splints, my crooked shorter leg, so I was completely bent at the waist, making the line of my belt slant downward from the right to the left hip.

I was considered a bright and smart child, though somewhat taciturn. People often told mother that they frequently saw me wandering aimlessly around the outskirts of town. I admit: my body trembled, my eyes feverishly searched for something, foam used to break out on my quivering lips because I was constantly listening to some voices inside me and was ashamed of the squeaking of the iron joints on my orthopedic device. The voices were human, some snakes were chasing me, and I was flying and flying, never hitting the bottom. Then I would wake up, with beads of sweat on my forehead, feeling like I was burning, and my body would be paralyzed. I would crouch in a corner, looking into the distance.

I wondered: was I asleep, or was I just lost in thought?

I also knew how to be different an ingenious and skillful teller of dirty jokes, a cheerful and joyous man, a liar when necessary, and honest to the point of tears, an actor listened by everyone with admiration: speaking in a rough and drawn-out tone, using a dialect understood only by those from that area, choosing words suitable for local follies. My face would then have a deliberately stupid expression, and my whole body would lean strangely towards the good leg that carried all its weight. People would clutch their bellies and beg me to stop so their guts wouldn't burst and fly out. I had a strong character, but I was already tormented by doubts, and I began to lean towards gloomy thoughts, philosophizing, and daydreaming. I often sat for hours on the floor, under the table in the kitchen, thinking that the world was as imperfect, sad, and miserable as this self-torment with no benefit to be drawn from it.

I spent the whole morning reminiscing about my childhood and early youth until the lengthened shadows marked the late hours and forced me to finally get up and prepare something for dinner before going to bed.

During the evening, I suddenly felt a tremendous urge to laugh. Certain sentences I had almost forgotten began to come alive within me, starting to twist my lips a little bit and compelling me to listen to them louder in their dialectal form. I must admit that it took considerable effort for me to bring to mind the individual faces that uttered them, making them anthology-worthy to me. I felt like searching in my bar to see if there was any wine or brandy left to treat myself as I so nicely revived some memories, but I instantly feared that it might blur the humor of what I approached quite tactfully like one of the toys that could break at any moment.

With a fork in one hand, on which a piece of steak was impaled, and a glass of blackberry juice in the other, I walked around the room from corner to corner, diagonally, so as to let myself imagine around me the whole fine pack with whom I sometimes used to greet the morning hammered.

As it seemed to me now, they were all here, only invisible, which did not bother me at all in communicating with them, on the contrary, in my ears echoed their sentences that I had chosen and adapted to my current mood, which again was a cruel consolation for being abandoned by them for years. I dared not think about that; I was now grateful to them for what I had realized: that both tragedy and comedy grow in the same soil and can replace one another in an instant.

Then I heard the doorbell. I put the glass and the fork down, hesitated for a moment, and listened to see if anyone outside could have heard my recent comical outburst. I held my breath for a bit, feeling my heart pounding so hard I could hear it beating in my neck too. I had the impression someone was standing at the door, waiting for my invitation to enter. I certainly wanted to know who it could be at this time of the night, knowing that everyone was aware of my unsociability, so I was all the more surprised by the bell that announced the uninvited guest. I do not say that, given my nature, I was vexed by this, I even believe I felt something akin to joy at the prospect of talking to someone and passing the time just when I subconsciously wanted it.

I took a step with my healthy leg and asked right away: "Who's there?"

There was no answer.

I didn't want to open the window; I was constantly haunted by a dream in which I saw myself beheaded at the window as I wanted to see who was calling me there. As soon as I poked my head out, something heavy and sharp, like a guillotine, fell on my neck. Even today, although I don't consider myself superstitious, I feel that right away something heavy and sharp would fall on my neck if I stuck my head out the window.

I repeated once more: "Who's there?"

Silence. Now I no longer had the impression that it was someone who wanted to talk with me. Fear prevented me from moving my left leg too, and I stood, somewhat grotesquely, on my right leg like a heron sensing danger from somewhere. I was able to think like that until the moment when from afar spread the combined laughter and shouts of rascals, who wished me a good time, and, on top of that, called me a madman and a fool.

I instantly rushed to the door handle, moving clownishly at the hips. I opened the door and without hesitation or any caution, ran straight into the darkness towards those voices. I would not have forgiven myself if I had stayed in the apartment. I suddenly felt the urge to fight for my pride, for my dignity, for my place in this world, to chase someone, to break their ribs, instead of flatter by silence so that no one would touch or provoke me, causing me to suffer and put up with it.

Shaaaaaaaave! various tones of children's voices outbarked each other, probably referring to my beard.

And again, I was a man without trust, "the weirdo from that little house", who should be provoked just because he is such kind.

What kind? Well such!

I rush to the path. I see some lights turning on in the nearby houses in the neighborhood, I hear some voices, not knowing anymore where they're coming from, whether it's still those rascals or someone else shouting after me, mocking me, my leg, and I hear thousands of voices in a swarm, laughter flowing like a symphony, a terrible laughter, I cannot allow them to ridicule me like that. What bothers them about my silence, my resistance to not being among them? I would like to know where they are hiding, because I cannot accept the idea that I will now replace peace with chasing after children and their voices. I will catch every single one of them, just like Gulliver did with the Lilliputians. I hear them all around murmuring, making plans, snickering, half-whispering my nickname: Shave!, and as I am listening to that, I no longer feel any fear, but rush through the night like a witch on a broomstick, hearing the screeching of the unlubricated iron joints on my orthopedic device, and listening to Dr. Lukač's voice recommending spas to my mother, as many therapeutic baths as possible and everything will be fine, Mrs. Wollensky, only spas can help the child, spas are the best, I tell you, spas and only spas can help little Albert, and this fills me with such rage that I feel I could swallow earth and chew grass as if it were the best steak or chop. At that moment, I completely forget the frame of my life, I run across the line, and suddenly, I stop being an outsider. "Mrs. Wollensky, please fully trust in what modern medicine has achieved "I see that doctor's gash of a mouth opening and two thin lips moving. Mother is crying, but she is still careful not to hurt the doctor's vanity or his authority, so she doesn't know what to do out of confusion, and only wipes her tears, twisting her fingers with an ironed handkerchief. I feel my own strength and my own nature, and I know that I must overcome the illness. I watch my mother fold the paper with the doctor's diagnosis in Latin, which is all scribbled in a true doctor's handwriting.

Horror! Horror of God! – poor Ursula let an involuntary sigh escape her mouth, but she wouldn't want anyone to hear it, not even the Lord, who could easily punish and reproach her for such despondency. One must believe in His grace, in His mercy, misericordia, one must always believe in Him, for His Wrath and His vengeance are tremendous; life is about defeating the devil, and God is so merciful that He sees everything, forgives, and helps. Poor Ursula constantly pondered what she might have done to incur the Lord's wrath on her child, and then the unfortunate woman brought back from memory that she had once cheated on her husband-the-despot and completely forgot about it, but now she remembered. She was now reminded of it by her son's polio, *poliomyelitis pedis sinistri, nervi peronei*. Since then, she never found comfort, except that she put her son under protection from those who spoke unkindly about him, and even from those who kept silent in the presence of those who did not think well of her Albi.

Silence is approval she used to say.

I was still listening to the voices, but now already exhausted, with a damp forehead and sweaty back, I collapsed by the street, and then managed to take a few more steps to reach a tree and take a breather, so my heart wouldn't jump out of my chest. I kept my hands on my hips, leaning my head against the tree. I lifted it and cried out into the blackness of the sky towards the unknown boy: "If you do this again, I'll kill you!"

Why did I feel that no one in the world was happier than me when the teacher at school gave me the role of a valet in "Uncle Tom's Cabin" with just one line: "Here they come". I recited it for Oscar, because I knew precisely how that line should be delivered, considering I heard it in childhood when my mother and I would visit the clinic once a year for my bad leg check-up. I know it was always terribly cold and that I trembled from who knows what, the cold, fear, or something else? People came early to get in line and waited even longer for the examination to start until someone would notice and whisper: "Here they come!"

And I remembered something else while I was coming to myself and catching my breath. I recalled how I perfected my French, shedding my local accent by uttering the words more quietly and slowly: La télévision, diffusion de France Paris. Le cabinet de la consultation. Monsieur Dimon qui allait souvent à Paris faisait volontiers des commissions pour ses voisins. Le cabinet de la consultation...

IX

WE WERE AFRAID OF EACH OTHER, AND WE BOTH TRIED TO GET CLOSER TO EACH OTHER BECAUSE LIFE WAS EMPTY FOR BOTH OF US, AND ISN'T MAN A BIG QUESTION TO HIMSELF THEN?

It was indeed an unusual moment when that young policeman, with his legs apart, stood in front of me in the darkness. To some extent, I could interpret his insolence on the basis of what I had heard about them, but I did by no means approve of his behavior, which, by the way, did not encourage or comfort me at all.

There was complete silence all around, the barking of a dog could be heard from somewhere, and the muezzin was calling the azan.

The policeman asked who I was, what I was, and why I had gotten off at that very station. Oh, God, even that? Yes, he specifically said that word – "very", which immediately caught my ear because I instantly thought that surely no stranger ever disembarks or stays here, except to quickly fill a bottle with water from the station tap and then run off. It was all too clear that by using this word, he immediately let me know that there was something quite suspicious about a man he had never seen before getting off the train, and now he rightfully expected an answer that would certainly not satisfy or appease him. The arrival of a stranger probably draws attention in this area, if not even a sensation, hence such curiosity at the very first step.

I told him that I had gotten off the train completely by chance, deliberately avoiding to mention the young lady from the compartment, as I believed that could bring even more trouble upon me. The man in front of me had the face of a thug. I wasn't even sure what the face of a thug should look like because one day, for who knows what reasons, I might become a thug myself, and I wonder what my face would look like then and whether it would become thuggish just because I had committed a thuggish act. I only wondered what that could have to do with what I had imagined a moment earlier. I thought: here lies a new, foreign, and unknown world.

He asked to see my documents, at which he directed the beam of his flashlight. He checked my first and last names, reading them syllable by syllable in a relaxed manner, and then, when we both somehow agreed that I was indeed Albert Wollensky (that's what I say, but that's not what's written in the papers), he calmly ordered me to come with him to the police station. In his movements, there was a touch of that cruelty and insane austerity, something abnormal that a uniform evokes in a man, keeping him constantly excited, tense, and clownishly ridiculous.

I had to go with him, but I didn't let him hold my hand because that would mean that I was either caught or highly suspicious. Even as it was, my situation was more than pathetic, and I almost pitied myself for getting into this mess, completely innocent, and I felt a desire to renounce all human pride. A vague thought swirled in my head – hyper- dimensionally that they were not allowed to do anything to me as long as I was outside and while some of the passers- by could see us, but that they would beat me, perhaps even kill me, as soon as they took me in there. I didn't dare to shout, considering that such an action could give them the right to unleash upon me what my previously polite behavior had forced them to restrain. I regarded this man as a monster and would never be able to understand how I could continue to walk calmly beside him. Luckily for me, there weren't many passers-by to see us at that time, so I myself quickened my pace to reach our destination sooner.

I knew I had done nothing wrong, not even thought of anything bad (except for that strange association with the face of a thug), so they couldn't take anything amiss, and thus I was even more puzzled why fear gripped me the entire way and, with some pious demeanor, I was trying to appear as humble as a nun, without even daring to ask him to give me my documents back, let alone protest about this farce he was putting me through. I knew that no one could deny me that right, but I would rather recommend it to someone else in a similar situation as my suggestion than allow that right to myself. I thought: perhaps it's better to keep quiet, and they will let me go when they see I'm harmless. Moreover, I was obsessed with the idea that they might actually want this in order to find a valid reason to beat and thrash me pitilessly, so I didn't want to give them such satisfaction by protesting loudly. I decided to remain cold and distant, indifferent, not to look as if I were mocking them, no! but rather to appear ostensibly courteous and meek, I mean, not so unpleasant or conceited so that it would not turn out that insolence, that is, offense is the best defense – but what did I, dear God, have to defend myself from when I was not guilty of anything, nor did I believe these fools would blame me. It cannot be said that I was calmer because of this, because experience had taught me that a person was never safe from anyone or anything. The only certainty is that one will die, the rest is avoidance and prayers to God that nothing hits you on the head.

The way things were, it looked like everything was going to be fine.

- How come you got off the train at this very place when your ticket is valid for further travel? He insisted again.
- I don't know I replied. I think I meant to return home.

That seemed to satisfy him, so he fell silent and didn't ask me anything else for the rest of the way.

At the station, I was interrogated by an old station commander. I found out later that his name was Krsto. He was quite different from that presumptuous officer. In all likelihood, he questioned me for about thirty minutes. He must have concluded from my answers that I was just an ordinary and harmless person. From his smile towards the end of our conversation, I deduced that he probably considered me scatterbrained and innocuous, so he gave me a lecture full of pathos, strict, fatherly and solemn, advising me not to do it again, because – I myself must admit getting off at a station without a strong reason, especially when I have no relatives here, was, to say the least, inappropriate and more befitting someone I wouldn't dare to name.

- Whom? – I instantly fired back.
- Whom? He was surprised by my inappropriate question, but he didn't find any reason to get seriously angry about it. Figure it out yourself, thank God, you're not a child!

Nevertheless, it was the best thing he could say for both of us. I cannot say it flattered my vanity. I had to take into account where I was and in what situation I was told that. Now, the most important thing was that they couldn't do anything to me nor did they intend to. Everything else was less important.

Still, when I exited through the main entrance and saw that it wasn't yet dawn, I felt somewhat strange, a bit uncomfortable, and a bit comical.

Guys, if my mom could see me I recalled the words from the Blue Racer cartoon.

The first thing I did was go to the train station to inquire when the next train was. I saw that it was only in the afternoon.

I didn't know where to go, I looked around and was convinced that, wherever I went, it would be interesting, even though I had never even heard of the name of this place, let alone knew anything about it. I didn't deny that I had some sort of luck getting off the train here, because I immediately noticed that it was picturesque, full of greenery and trees, and besides, I saw the first peasants in folk costumes which completely fascinated and captivated me. Obviously, I had strong reasons to be happy that my train was only in the afternoon, and I probably would have been even more satisfied had I been able to extend my visit and stay for a few more days.

As the locals passed by me, I listened to their words, mostly verbs they directed at each other to draw attention to something. "Watch out!", "Don't!", "Go!", "Wanna smok'?"

I cannot claim that there wasn't some harmony in it, and that they didn't perform it with a particular style, which had to touch me and leave an indelible impression on me. I sympathized with their little horses, so heavily laden that it was simply impossible to believe they could even carry it, and thus, I felt certain disgust at their heartlessness towards the poor animals.

I had to feel wretched as I stood aside, watching the columns of people and horses pass through the middle of the street. What surprised me the most though, was that none of them returned my gaze.

Still, the thought imposed itself on me that what I was seeing I had seen somewhere before. My head was spinning, I couldn't remember, and I seriously considered giving up on that futile endeavor, but whenever I decided to focus on something else, the thought of what had just been in my sight treacherously returned and disturbed me even more. Nothing could bring me to my senses. I continued to see familiar faces, which astounded me. I thought I might soon run out of breath. There's no doubt I was walking through familiar scenes from one of my dreams, which I recounted to Tereza right after waking up. There was no longer any question that what I saw, I had already seen in the mentioned dream. I suppose it could easily be the imagination which always works intensely when the senses are heated, but in my firm belief, this was not about any new image, but rather about a new experience and feeling of that image. Out of excitement, I began to laugh so uncontrollably and boldly, contorting my face into grimaces so much that I believe those who were watching me must have thought I was one of those who are *already* or are *going ga-ga*.

X

FRIGHTENED, I DRAW A CIRCLE AROUND MYSELF. (WHOEVER NEEDS THE DEVIL, BUT FEARS HIM, SECURES THEMSELVES WITH A CIRCLE)

I slept too little, so I used the night for reading and writing. This made me quite angry, mainly because of my overloaded senses, which were constantly tense, giving me no peace, so I felt like a wound-up clock in an infernal machine most of the time. I also used to tease myself, joking at my own expense. I did this with such style that, without false modesty, I could easily categorize it as brilliant acting. In doing so, I took into account the circumstances under which I was only willing to accept such a comedy. What I once used to make others laugh, condemn, or mock them, I now generously applied to myself. It seems to me that in those moments I had a very clear desire to be guided by my imagination and to regain some sort of faith in dreams, which I had pretty much lost. I was afraid of embarrassing myself before myself, as I was then a strict and implacable judge. All this crossed my mind while the words were still boiling within me, so it must have especially moved me and made me feel a bit spoiled. I believed that both joy and fear were emerging from within me, which influenced my desire to repeat the experience more often, of course, when I was capable and in the mood for it.

I clearly remember one conversation with myself. At first, nothing promised a dialogue. I was mumbling the words of a song, then began to deliver a farewell speech fit for some great buffoon at the moment he was about to leave this world. I tried to capture the gift of speech with paradoxical turns at the moment he uttered the historic sentence: "I don't have the words to express all the pain, all the sorrow accumulated these days since we learned that the inevitable death this time too, etc. etc. etc.", so I wanted to change it to: "...we all think you died, but I know well, you taught us that it cannot be true and that this is one of your great jokes on us. We've learned enough from you not to fall for such tricks, because we know, and we know well, that at the moment we are here sniveling and lamenting, you would get up, and it would be enough for us to hear your ironic: Humph! See, you won't catch us doing that, so on the occasion of your death, I will say: We have gathered to make another comedy and once again forget that we are alive. You can leave us, we can even bury you here, but know that none of us present believes you have left and that you want to do so. You don't even have to return that's your personal matter but you will remain among us, and memory is the greatest reward that a person can receive from people."

Is it really so?

I read and write a lot. I spend most of my time with books that lead me to something unusual and shrouded in mystery, which is inaccessible, restrained, and not easily revealed to my senses and which intensifies my desire to once again, as at the beginning of my life, know nothing and to free myself, to eliminate the experience that is just a burden and prevents me from truly, truly enjoying. I hope that somehow I will manage to find the key to my depravity, in which, it seems, demons also have a role, and I lately feel they are increasingly leading me by the nose, hovering around me and mocking me.

To begin with, that much was clear to me, that is, only as much as they gave me a reason to think so. I often had to turn towards the wall to avoid looking at the interior of the room, so I wouldn't see them as ghosts walking, hovering, or grinning at me from each and every corner. Terrified, I constantly expected one of them to place a hairy hand on my shoulder (I don't know why I imagined those hands as particularly hairy) and to warn me that it is neither nice nor polite to welcome guests in such a manner.

What is nice and polite when it comes to them? Is it nice and polite that they don't greet me, although they enter my house, and after a while, I hear them leaving, descending the stairs. I look out the window and see them flying away, then disappearing into the tops of the poplar trees. Now I know why the leaves rustle in them. When day comes again, I find myself exhausted, tired from something, although I haven't done anything physical, and the accumulated sorrow simply tears me apart, causing an awful tension.

Then I couldn't help but remember the times when I was still working as a teacher at school, namely, the classroom events, the grimacing faces in front of me, every single one having dark eyes in which I saw misfortune and misery, the drunkenness of their fathers and the madness of their mothers, the locked food, the money hidden in-between the wardrobe items, the first tattoos on the biceps, the names of some equally unfortunate girls who gave themselves over to them and lost their virginity, the first slaps by jealous gentlemen under some lampposts with the sixty-volt light meagerly dripping from it; all of them together were holding my hands, and the rest were grinning in my face, and then I felt that one of them was pounding me, and masterfully at that, hitting me right in the plexus. I think that was when I realized that life is often the annulment of another life, the negation, the unquenchable and irrational will for violence that can never be satisfied but only reinforced in its conviction.

The children amused themselves at my expense, seeing nothing unusual in it. They were driven by a wave of frenzy and hatred, not so much towards me, but towards the chair on which I was sitting, so they thought to push it away too, perhaps because it bothered them that I was resting my rear on it. Their eyes gained a colorless shine, and their gaze was also full of sorrow, so they no longer had to try to appear wanton.

- Don't touch me! I yelled, feeling that this wouldn't end well. Don't you dare come a step closer!

Next to me, a book with a text full of restraint, like a letter to be searched with excitement and joyful hope. I'm thinking: no one was restrained back then, everything was so obvious, we just didn't know what the end would be. Just like the detective stories I never valued.

I cannot quite remember the moment when the boy with the cynical expression on his face started hitting me on the head, and I couldn't think of anything better than to close my eyes and wait for the end of this assault.

I stare into the semi-darkness, completely filled with rage. In front of me, I see again that young man, whose neck is all spindly, his eyes reddened like a rabbit's, and his pants disgustingly clinging to his muscular legs, thus making prominent his enormous penis with balls like a bull's.

Yes, I remember thinking as he was hitting me in the face: What do declensions look like, and will there be a future perfect or present conditional in a subordinate clause for *concordance des temps*, because for heaven's sake the action of the subordinate clause happens simultaneously with the action of the main clause; there, that's the proper literary French without which General De Gaulle wouldn't have deigned to give anyone his attention. He would refuse to read a telegram about war declaration if he knew that the imperfect was replaced with the ordinary present. God, what audacity and ignorance! Outrageous! Scandalous!

What use are books? What use are writers? What use, after all, is human thought when it only makes a person sadder and more fragile? It is needed by those who would seek it out and find it even if it weren't offered to them. To those who don't need it, it appears like a tight grip around their necks, it doesn't let them live and it doesn't guarantee them anything concrete.

I uttered this crap provoked by the event of three years ago when everything came crashing down on me, and I seriously considered ending it all by taking my own life without accusation and much fuss and disappearing from this evil and unjust world. That I say I thought most seriously about and I would have surely done it if I hadn't received a letter from the school the next day in which those school fags wrote that I was suspended from work by the decision of the Working People's Assembly 10:9 because I provoked student Ivan Vilenica with my inappropriate behavior and thereby directly caused the disruption of normal, friendly and professional communication between the class and myself. I had the right to appeal within the legal term of 8 (eight) days, etc., stamp, signature...

Oh, God! I made my room into a theater of antiquity, and my anger and my unhappiness into an ancient drama, that is, a monodrama.

Oh, God! I was looking at the ceiling and I thought that perhaps one fly, which was napping upside down on it, was God. I wanted to laugh at the fly, but I stopped instantly, thinking that it wasn't a fly after all. If it's not a fly, but God, I believe it might as well be the devil. This, then, is our eternal reckoning. And the next day, another letter will arrive, I already see the header with the name of the publishing house to which I sent the manuscript of a collection of poems in the neo-futurism style two years ago. The editor kindly informs me that my manuscript has been rejected and that he sincerely hopes that our cooperation will continue. Of course, he wishes me better luck next time. Something similar to a kind lottery show host. Acts of kindness and smiles from ear to ear. Splendid!

XI

MAN IS HIS OWN SUPPORT AND HIS OWN ABYSS

It is understandable that for a woman sleeping with her own child is the end of the world. This has always been my natural opinion, and I would be greatly mistaken if I denied that I had never thought about it and that I had not been somehow particularly excited about it. I will never be able to understand three things: fagdom, drugs, and incest. I always felt a secret quiver in my throat whenever I heard that someone had done it, and it often happened that in my anger I would turn to comedy, and it seemed to me that I achieved a better effect. Then I suddenly realized that comedy serves no other purpose than to entertain or annoy, because – in essence it is the weapon of the helpless. I do not believe that it can change anything, although comedians have always been angrier than those who convey everything seriously and unequivocally. Comedy, especially one with a higher meaning, does not reach anyone's ears, so comedians have to come to terms with the fact that they are alone and that they are "telling stories to the deaf", and that no normal person cares about them unless their joke improves the digestion of the audience. Comedy is a performance and not an invitation to stop it in real life.

Thus, over time, I completely changed my opinion on how to treat what deserves disgust and public condemnation. My mood changed to the extent that I began to increasingly feel pain and anger, which made my heart beat harder and faster. It was probably then that I started distancing myself from people, falling into what is usually called despair. It was around this time that I began my autobiography, which initially had the working title *A Brief Excursion into the World of My Memories*. It was difficult, everything was somehow tangled, even though I approached the text with considerable tenderness from the start. Over time, I stopped expecting the writing to bring me comfort; on the contrary, as the manuscript progressed, it brought me more and more misery and dissatisfaction, and it simply urged me to abandon this futile task, because I would never achieve my ultimate goal if I sought justification for myself, as if I were at least a defeated general or a former president of the state writing his memoirs and seeking an apology before posterity and history. Not to go too far, I will say that I was prompted to take this step by two evident facts: the negative vibrations that I felt emanating from everyone towards me, especially from my closest ones father, sister, and uncle who were constantly advising and pestering me, and demons who appeared to me more and more frequently, especially at night. During the day, they probably didn't dare to show up.

There was a pronounced urge in me to prove that society condemned me to suspension from work with a 10:9 vote because I negatively vibrated towards that prick of a boy and directly influenced his Neanderthal behavior. Indeed, I am looking for a way to renounce this world since fear prevents me from finally departing from it. I want to live with wistfulness in my soul and to welcome those who call upon the saints to visit me. I don't have the impression that I hope this will truly come to pass, but at least I entertain the thought that it is still sometimes worth believing in that little piece of heaven, which so far seemed to me still untainted by my bad experience.

One evening, Tereza burst into my room, and from the doorway, keeping the door wide open, tearfully said that mom had just died. She collapsed in the armchair while listening to music from the radio. Heart attack.

- *Zis too befalls zee person* father concluded over dinner. He insisted on being the first on the list of the bereaved family,

and only then the two of us. I saw something shameful in it and asked that my name be left out.
- *Schame on ya* – father said *she sacrificed for ya zee most. Ya did zis to her.*

I didn't respond. It was quite clear to me that her waving from the window today, as a sign of welcome, was the last memory I had of her. She was at the far window in a blue muslin dress. Since then, I have felt a particular tenderness towards the color blue.

She now flickers before my eyes, though in a somewhat blurry outline, which nonetheless made me feel a moment of bliss due to her presence. It seems to me that a smile of happiness spread across my lips because she was here, beside me. Who knows, that's how it seems. If I had a mirror before me, I would certainly check if it was a smile of recollection or resigned acceptance: Yes, that's how a person leaves.

I spoke with Tereza, completely indifferent to what she had just told me. I think I would have remained just as cold if father hadn't appeared at the door, asking her to go back to him and help with mother. As I watched him, small and stocky, having neither neck nor waist, Tereza suddenly snapped me out of my distraction: "Albert, you surely reproach, despise and reject me by acting this way towards me, don't you?"

I looked at her with genuine astonishment.
- It's pointless to pretend you don't understand me
- she continued.
- What do you mean, Tereza? – I asked. I really don't know what you're talking about.
- Then it doesn't even matter she said. It's best when one doesn't know anything.

I wanted to ask her what it was that I didn't know when I knew everything, when everything was clear to me, except for the fact why mother had to die today. What did her waving at me mean: a greeting or a threat that I would be alone in the future?

Tereza was about to say something, but father screamed from the door: *"Will ya come here already, four- eyes?"*

She jumped as if released from the spring. She went out into the hallway, not forgetting to close the door behind her.

XII

LIFE. COINCIDENCE, PAIN, A SMILE, AND IA STRANGER AMONG STRANGERS

Only now I realize that I should never have allowed myself to open for anyone the door to my intimate life. I will give up trying to explain how much strength I lacked to awaken desire for someone, especially a woman, because I believed that by awakening such feelings, I would discover something entirely new in myself. I believed that there is something terribly hypocritical in the urge in a man's instinct, all the more so since he is able to successfully restrain it and skillfully hide it, which again is not in the least characteristic of an animal. I talked about this only once with Tereza, although I always feared such and similar conversations, keeping a distance like a monk.

I would usually choose such kind of conversation, and that "conversation", as a rule, always remained the same repetition of the insinuation that all people are the same all made of flesh and blood and thus all having the same physiological needs. I was, of course, referring to normal people; the sick were not the subject here.

I deliberately avoided the word: intentions, because it I believe would immediately put me in the awkward position of having to defend myself against dishonorable thoughts, so I preferred ambiguous words. I couldn't agree with myself whether I was acting to be a steadfast person in front of myself or acting in front of her, playing an honorable person.

She initially accepted my words without objection, and I interpreted this as her habit of listening to me to the end and probably for giving me for everything. Additionally, upon returning from Romance studies, I found her with ten- month-old Adrian, without a husband or his last name, completely devoted to her son, always watching over him, except when he was sleeping, with those tear-burnt eyes. I'm sure she watched over him even in her sleep. With a hundred percent certainty, the doctors had already determined that the boy would be retarded, deliberately avoiding the words feeble-minded, cretin, imbecile, idiot and that there would be no cure for it for the rest of his life.

For the first time, we started digging into our family genealogy, and it was soon discovered that Tereza, of course without her or her husband's knowledge, had married her third cousin on her mother's side. The crossover of chromosomes is relentless. What a coincidence: choosing a cousin as a husband from among half a million men, getting all five numbers in the lottery, and being born from among 400,000 of father's spermatozoa, reaching the goal and coming into this world, well, that's called a coincidence. Considering that I, such a frail, fool, bungler and scoundrel, managed to tower over all of them, I could only imagine the kind of constitution my unborn brothers would have.

Tereza's happiness burst like an overinflated balloon. She completely neglected her studies in classical philology. The little knowledge of languages she had helped her get a job at a tourist bureau. Her husband Emil tried to pin all the blame on her, but she met him with silence and a willingness to suffer. He constantly took the opportunity to pester her with stories about her branch of the lineage being miserable and hermaphroditic, claiming that she didn't take the effort to warn him in time about the danger of inbreeding, and that it was all her fault for bringing them to this point.

And she believed she no longer had any right to mock anyone, so I think it was then that she decided not to ridicule anyone again, let alone someone's misfortune or loneliness.

I always envied her a little for the nonchalance with which she was closing the door behind her; in the same self- satisfied manner in which others open them, because they go among the people. She was entering the world where only her son awaited her. I'm sure he was quite enough for her. Her entire life revolved around that creature, in the bad sense of the word. While her husband wandered the world to atone for or forget the committed sin, she except when she was at work spent all her time in her room with her son, teaching him poems, to recite them as nicely and articulately as possible, to know the capitals of all the countries of the world, and preferably to answer as quickly as a shot, something she demanded with special pride he demonstrate in front of guests.

There was something sad and obscene in that circus where she showed off her drill in front of people, who were only able to split their chops into a fake smile, as an unquestionable sign of the child's intelligence. And she believed her son could understand and do everything, even learn to tell in time about his number two, but he still couldn't manage to say his own name: "I'm Adrian".

In the midst of Ouagadougou, Paramaribo, Kingston, something sweetish would start to stink in the air, the fake smiles would start to sour, and Tereza would feel a wave of shame, despair, and depression because things were as they were and nothing else. It's futile to lie and deceive oneself. Dogs and cats find sand to urinate in and then bury the moisture. If only I had given birth to them, it would have been easier for me. After one similar thought, she bit her tongue until it bled, thinking she had finally managed to bite it off.

So many times she had sworn to herself that she would never marry again, not only because she considered herself defiled, but because she believed she was unworthy of any man.

I lived not far from her. I even tried to joke with her, but she would often repay my futile effort with a grateful, contrived smile. I had the intention of taking her hand and holding it for hours. Otherwise, if I let go, she would wish to burn in her own hell as quickly as possible.

In front of me, she searched for an appropriate expression for what she was convinced as being inevitably destined for her, so she told memore than once that the question of her fate had long been decided, it was just not yet known who or what would finish her off. "Who knows, you might kill me one day" she once said. "And afterwards, let whoever wants to worry about which circle of hell to place me in."

Only then would I see her smile, but this time it wasn't contrived; it was entirely genuine, and it made her so beautiful that I couldn't help but regret the cruel fate that had befallen her. At that moment, it truly seemed to me that there was no more beautiful woman in the world, nor had there ever been such a beauty that I simply cannot describe the nostalgia and sadness I remember her with; this is the only remaining thing that is still beautiful and dear to me and that almost brings tears to my eyes.

I can hardly remember some details that are meant to prove that my love for her had something physiological as well, which, of course, I was very successfully hiding. I strictly limited myself, starting with the look in which only an attentive eye would be able to sense some sort of desire, and ending with the wish to masturbate while thinking of her. The passion grew so much within me that I increasingly ignored the shame of incest, which she had already experienced to some extent with our distant relative, but at the same time I wanted to remain alone, withdrawn, so that I could not touch anyone and cause them pain. Naturally, it was a huge effort and physical suffering on my part. Since then, everything started to tire me out.

- Do you read? Our family doctor asked me.
- No, reading tires me out.
- Do you watch television?
- No, it's too noisy.
- I see you have a telescope. Do you stargaze?
- No. The Earth spins, so that too tires me out.
- What, then, do you suffer from?
- I have a problem.
- Which problem?
- My dick is down to my knees.

I lay face down on the bed, with a pillow pulled over my head, thinking how grand words never uttered grand truths. Conquests are made with small, quiet, and serious ones. I thought about how history changes, how regimes change, how nearly all emperors have disappeared, how wealth will melt, how the Sun once revolved around the Earth and now the Earth revolves around the Sun, how God once existed and today he doesn't, but maybe he will exist again, how freedom was once the greatest treasure and today the greatest evil, how a man of today lives only one life, whereas in the past he lived two lives, and once – earlier still he lived several lives, how it is wrong to love out of pity or hate out of passion, I remembered telling mom not to buy a chair because her lap was the best place for me, I thought that writing was a purely personal matter, I recalled a cabaret singer with a deep voice from excessive smoking who popped my cherry one winter night on a broken ottoman, I thought about Christ, I thought about indestructible legends and remembered that singer again, gathering her things in the morning, putting on lipstick in front of a shard of a mirror, while I, ready to flee, stood in front of her, confused and undecided like a wuss, then I told myself that the downfall of humanity would be done by human hands and not someone's revenge God's or Satan's but solely man's, I convinced myself that I did not depend on the society and did not need its attention because I possessed inner freedom and inner peace, and then, the image of my uncle appeared before me, who, as soon as he ran a red light in Rome, swore to the carabiniere that he was indeed the president of a municipality in Yugoslavia and that it would be inconvenient if he was fined as he would use his authority, I remembered reading a newspaper survey about the city's TV program where a citizen complained about too few sex films, too few comedies for the working people to laugh at during the economic crisis, too little sport, and too much philosophy, well, I remembered this the one who complained was a shift leader in the finishing phase at the forestry company, and after that I remembered dear God, one can remember so many things I remembered that the fourth item on the agenda of an ancient school meeting was about procuring wood for the janitor...

The fear that someone would discover my torment pushed me more and more towards solitude, so I constantly sought reasons and proof before myself that I truly wanted to be alone, avoiding throwing off the burden by having the balls to shout: "Rezika, don't you see how much I love you? Why did God want you to be my sister?"

I conveniently uttered this in solitude so that it didn't even seem obscene to me. I even used to say it inwardly at moment I stood before her, but when she would say to me: "Albert, Albert, you surely reproach, despise or reject me by acting this way towards me, don't you? "all of my previous courage would instantly be gone until I heard her say again: "I know you're accusing me and that you have already turned your back on me. I'm not complaining; I deserved it."

I saw the lines between her eyebrows deepen. I continued to stand before her, silent. She probably thought I had nothing to say because I had already accused her. I, however, was astonished at myself for not saying aloud what I had so masterfully articulated inwardly a moment earlier with effective accent and intonation, to the point that I had opened my room door and walked over to repeat it to her, word for word. It seemed that I had even inhaled a bit more air and held it in my lungs just so that my voice would be deep and convincing.

I know that my father, in relation to me, followed the trait that all the Wollenskys have, which is that they are relentless and uncompromising when it comes to upbringing, because my God! It doesn't take much for a child to lose balance and fall into the abyss. This trait also served them as a convenient opportunity to fully express their audacity, rudeness and intolerance, so from a very young age, at the word up bringing or even someone's advice, I could immediately, in good conscience, pull out anything a gun, a stick, a stone, a knife and inflict pain. I never felt the tenderness of a teacher or concern for my mental hygiene in those two hypocrisies; on the contrary, I constantly saw someone's self-indulgence with a slight insinuation about their experience, so I preferred to take it as a parody of their own seductiveness and goodness rather than interpreting it with some higher pedagogical goals. This suddenly became clear to me when I began to perceive seriousness as a caricature and caricature as the only objectivity in the true sense of the word. This thought was prompted by a reminder of an event that had almost slipped my memory and which came to me quite unexpectedly. I couldn't stop wondering why I accepted this memory with a smile on my face.

Whenever I completed a task, I was proud in front of my father, and I felt I had some right to be loudly praised and patted on the head as a reward. My father never used dialect but always tried to speak in the literary language, always carefully choosing his words, in which, despite his efforts and softening of his voice, he couldn't help but retain the Tyrolean accent inherited from my grandfather, a native Tyrolean, which was in addition somewhat softened, where voiceless sounds were eternally replaced by the voiced ones.

- *Vee Yugos are zee vorst and zee best folkz in zee worlz!*
- In the world?
- *Well, in zee worlz!*

I doubt my father had no certain difficulties with syntax, but I think it was precisely due to his Germanic character and will that he managed to overcome that handicap at school and even surpass everyone else in knowledge, both in terms of grammar and orthography. He was excited by spelling errors in official documents and didn't want to justify the tearful apology of his typist, who whined to him that she wasn't a language teacher but just an ordinary typist pounding on the typewriter what others dictated.

He never had a sense of humor. Sometimes he wanted to make a joke, but it wilted before it even blossomed; it was sad rather than refreshing, so everyone around him forced smiles and avoided his eyes, which floated as if in oil, and that unhealthy redness of his would blaze even stronger.

- *I don't know how to lay an egg, but I know vat a rotten one is!* he'd purse his lips, thinking he'd given the perfect answer to that silly girl who only knew how to cry when someone scolded her, and spend the rest of the time laughing her head off and blowing gum bubbles. It was only later that I read somewhere that Skerlić had said something similar. Why my father liked that so much and used it as his trump card against his typist will forever remain a mystery to me. Perhaps not even God Himself understands.

Our immediate relations were anything but friendly. I admitted to myself that I had a purebred and first-class tyrant in him, whose offspring I accidentally happened to be in the sea of 400,000 of his spermatozoa that boiling somewhere in the darkness of my mother's womb, in whose retort I spent seven months and eight days, and then emerged prematurely in the sweat of her body, entering this world without a sound. They say the young doctor, mute and bewildered, stood not knowing what to do with me, as purplish blue as indigo, and those would surely have been my only moments spent in this world had it not been for the midwife Margita (as my mother told me her name was), who remembered to give me air through her mouth, thus bringing me through the back door into this life, the autobiography of which I am now writing. Since then, I've always wondered why all midwives in the world aren't named Margita.

I couldn't live under the illusion that my father would ever be able to remove that stern expression from his face, which already looked like a patina, when talking to me about matters concerning my upbringing, to laugh broadly, hug me, and say: *"Alpert, am I not a brilliant aktor for character roles? Believe me ven I say zat I managed to impose all your frustrations on ya with my superb aktink."*

I often thought about this and prayed to God that he would say those sentences, at least as a linguistic gag, to have it come out of him like from some electronic robot since he couldn't genuinely feel it. I believed that I could extinguish a forest fire with my spit sooner than this world miracle would happen. This is what I felt while I still had some hope, but then, when I completely resigned myself to the fate of a child being heartlessly drilled like a horse or trained like a dog for some kennel show to give paw whenever someone wanted or to bark on command, I knew I was the loneliest creature in the world.

- In the world? I would try going back to irony.
- *Well, in zee worlz!* replied someone to me strictly and seriously.

His strictness could never inspire trust in me. It scared me above all and strengthened my feeling of being truly alone. I couldn't find a confidant in Tereza, because we were both well into puberty, so our preoccupations were more or less different. At that time, I hardly ever saw her. Once, I even heard father quietly threatening mother that he wouldn't finance a whore and her bastards, whom various vagabonds and riffraff, just like she was, would impregnate her with.
- What are you blabbering about, man? mother pleaded. Aren't you ashamed before God?
- *If ya vere aschamed of Him, ya vould not allow yer daughter to roll under zee bridge viz difovci!*[1]

It is likely that he would have learned some lessons on the baselessness of his strictness if he had opposite him a more energetic mother, who could have stood in the way between his raised hand and me or Tereza. I instinctively shielded my head with my hands so that his big fist wouldn't hit me. I loved life then, or rather, I didn't love it, but I was afraid to leave it through the same door I came in. Even then, something told me I would do something extraordinary but what? I would be, let's say, a genius, a brilliant criminal, a great playboy, I would be a cardinal, a pope, who would hold masses in stadiums filled with so many people and boost their morale with my ideas, celebrating brotherhood among people and self-restraint. I would also lie on my deathbed when my mother and father went for a walk. I would deliver a eulogy in my own honor, feeling that every living being on this planet was listening, listing countless merits and spreading the legend about myself. My real name wasn't even known, I didn't accept invitations to awards either, hiding behind a fake name and living alone in the woods just to spite my father, to finally make him come to his senses and fatherly hug me and hold me close, kiss me and caress my head, and I would cry with joy that this world miracle had finally happened. The happiest creature in the world.
- In the world?

---

[1] DIF State Institute for Physical Education; difovci – DIF students

- *Well, in zee worlz!*

I had to pay a great price of suffering for that illusion.

I only blamed myself for those crazy dreams.

As soon as I admitted that to myself, it became easier, I felt as if I had dived deep and now surfaced with a pearl shell.

This brought my father out of his rapture as well. I remember he was moved by the cold expression on my face, which was no longer surprised, nor delighted, nor confused by anything because it had already become indifferent to everything, and he was carried away by that impression and said to me quite spontaneously: *"Alpert, it seems to me zat ya have become a mature man. I sink it's time zee two of us talked like man to man."*

I believe he meant it most sincerely by the way he placed his huge palm on my shoulder like a tired lumberjack puts his hand on a tree to rest a little. I felt his hand on my shoulder as if a large colorful venomous snake had coiled up and was dying there. A chill ran through me, which I felt through the shivers running up my spine and spreading from my shoulder across my entire back. I thought he would immediately remove his hand, so I was even more surprised when he hugged me.

- *Isn't it so, Alpert?* he asked.

I looked at him. I saw the wrinkles around his eyes. The skin on his neck was wrinkled, I saw old age. I thought: the wolf has crouched, he feels his time is running out. Is forgiveness truly a magnanimous act? Forgetting or understanding?

- Okay! I replied reluctantly.

I maliciously expected him to be crushed by my philological impudence and indifference. He despised slang and argot from the core of his heart. I'm sure that was precisely the reason I answered him that way. Instead, I noticed wistfulness in his eyes. Perhaps it wasn't wistfulness, but the awakening that I had indeed become mature but also a dangerous man for him to occasionally dare to be cruel to me or my sister. I might have even felt sorry for him if I had allowed myself to listen to him.

- *Tomorrow is zee anniversary of mom's death* he said. *As usual, we'll all gazer for dinner. Zee poor sing has at least dezerved zat."

XIII

WITHOUT MY OWN WILL, I CAME INTO THE WORLD, AND THROUGHOUT MY LIFE, I OBSERVED EVERYTHING WITH ASTONISHED EYES, INCLUDING WHAT WAS HAPPENING BEFORE ME...

In the evening, before I fall asleep, I wish to dream of flowers. They say that if you see flowers in a dream, they will bring you joy.

Thus, the first guest who appeared in my dream was the Unholy One who emerged before me, appearing sometimes as a black beast, sometimes as a bear, and sometimes as a fleece less ram, and soon after, I heard them all speaking to me in unison, each in their own language and onomatopoeia, about wickedness as the only honorable endeavor worthy of every form of life, so I wondered where they got such thoughts from, and they told me that when everything pleasant to the body is forbidden in this world, and one must admit that what is pleasant to the body is also pleasant to the soul, what did we say, the bear asked the ram, but the fleece less ram remained silent, just occasionally nodding and emitting something that resembled bleating; something like that, but nothing like bleating at all, it was more like grunting, the first one only seemed like bleating to me because it was a ram and not a pig, and what else would you expect from a ram but to bleat and not to grunt, or perhaps it was all just an illusion, with the bear bleating or grunting, whatever?, ant the ram growling, the black beast... the black beast had no choice but to roar unless it had been the one bleating or growling earlier, and the ram barking, who knows who was making what sound, anyway, by my old bad habit, I continued to recall what I had seen with a feeling of an inevitable cold of melancholy, with which I watched all these lives entering church for the Mass, and the church was up on the hill, almost entirely bathed in the rosy glow of the evening summer sky, so I instantly thought I had to control myself and stay calm so they wouldn't notice me, as I would probably have to go to the priest's sermon too, but I have never believed in that, although I often deluded myself into thinking there was something sublime in it, but things always told me that I remained either cold and indifferent to it all or simply failed to find the charm, hence I continued to observe this biblical scene of obedience and couldn't in any way determine if all those creatures suddenly took off; I just saw them greasing chairs arranged for the sermon in the church, and they all mounted them and immediately flew up, covering almost the entire sky, and from that sight, I just thought the sky had darkened and perhaps this was the Judgment Day, and actually it was still daylight it just couldn't be seen because of the multitude of chairs, and the demons who were in a low flight from house to house, and the paralytic old men, women, and children, cured, came out of their homes with smiles on their faces, waving to the demons and their leader, who still appeared sometimes as a black beast, sometimes as a bear, and sometimes as a fleece less ram; the same people were bringing up from the cellars all the best food and drink they had for the healers, and then, suddenly, all those good-natured people, for whom I felt sincere affection and kindness, descended on their chairs, and with them was the one who then appeared in the form of a ram, who had to be a priest because he was bleating at the altar, and all those who followed and accompanied him turned into wolves, nothing but wolves, who immediately started howling so that I involuntarily laughed at this comical metamorphosis, and it seems that I even clapped in delight at the magic, and I made a clownish grimace, but then, I saw something incredible that I could not have anticipated, that this game could turn into something horrible, horrible... horrible, because suddenly, all those wolves in the pack started chasing the fleece less ram to devour him just as their unholy spirit had taught them, and this kept changing constantly, as the wolves turned back into demons, and the demons into people again, and it repeated until they reached a tall grass through which they only needed to pass to become invisible; the exception were the women who became mares, whose tails rose and their legs spread, and I concluded that those invisible demons had intercourse with them, from which they snorted and stood stiff like some statues of primitive artists, a man would say as if they were about to do a number two, one could only assume that it would take some time, because I watched it closely, drenched in sweat, and I could clearly recognize and hear their panting and I say whinnying, by which I concluded that they were a hundred percent comfortable and that they really were doing those things, and I was seized with such curiosity and gripped by some new powers so I couldn't remain restrained and cool, and soon I felt that stiff *fool* of mine between my legs as if I had mounted a pole; that's how I felt; indeed, the image was hypnotizing, even a little funny, but I still had infinite understanding, or rather, patience, for that comical situation, because it provoked a sexual ambiguity that, without a doubt, I could cling to, and even put up with it, since then I saw how the hind legs of the mares naturally came together and they began to chew hay and bread that someone invisible was offering them (I believe the same ones who had been riding them until a moment ago), yes, yes, you are brave, kudos to you for being able to endure all that, I couldn't bear to feel the cold semen inside me and for that chill to be fertilized within me and that I give birth to a cold creature, dear God, that is what I resent them for because I'm afraid of demons, I'm terribly afraid that demons will come to me like that and want to do similar things to me, if not the same things, then something similar, which looks like this, for instance, when I saw them all together both the mares and the invisible ones transformed into moths, then into chickens, then into cats, and all together, amidst a great noise, they ran to the gathering, each taking their place on one of the nearby trees or on the rocks, and in the middle stood my nephew, yes, my nephew, that idiot Adrian, who was to be sacrificed, and instantly one moth left that crowd, a big, huge, enormous garden carpet (xanthorhoe fluctuata), and landed on the idiot attaching itself over his heart, yeah, and covered his entire left side with its contrasting white wings, what I want to say is that it was a good match since he was all dressed in black and a lot of other things happened, until Adrian's head dropped and he crumpled to the ground; now everyone knew that it was from the sting of that enormous garden carpet, so without a doubt I would have understood the whole case if the garden carpet's wings did not start to shrink so that only the body remained, and it looked like a caterpillar, which suddenly turned into a being with a human body in which I recognized my sister Tereza, who instantly squatted, then knelt on her knee and put her little finger in the hole she had made in Adrian's heart as a garden carpet moments earlier, and those present huffed three times and shook their heads as a sign that they fully approved of what she had done, thus showing her all the signs of respect, and then the one who they considered to be the leader stood out from the crowd and everyone else gathered closely around him, paying more respect to him than to Tereza, and, a bit later, as a sign of respect, everyone kissed his naked buttocks, or even that thing, which was under his tail, licking at the same time his exhausted body and thereby once again acknowledging him as their one and only true teacher and master, although everyone felt that it must be something probably unworthy of a human being and that it was a kind of shame, especially if done in secret as they did, and not publicly, so I too began to feel their embraces and kisses, their eyes shone like sulfur fire, and unwillingly I found myself at the center of their attention, I admit, mostly due to my own recklessness, which initially caused some confusion and even amazement among them, thus revealing to me that my smile had grown into a smirk, which I felt clearly in my soul and on my lips, yes, that's how it was, I remember I began nodding, terribly unhappy, and gazing rigid with horror at the thought that I could do what they did, or at least wish to do it, or ultimately resign to fate and actually do it. Dear God, would that then be me or would I become what I truly am: finding the courage to do what I sometimes most sincerely think and no longer having dreams about that horrible and disgusting tribunal, conducting the court hearing and thundering from the judge's bench that, following the customs of the ancestors, I must have God before my eyes, and according to their final judgment, which is already written, they declare, proclaim, decide, and decree that I have finally sold my soul to the devil and that I deserve appropriate measures of retribution, that is, the strictest punishment; the gavel strikes the bench, the hearing may be considered closed, it is the month of April, in the year of our Lord nineteen hundredth since the birth of Christ, and after that in the eighty-first year, God, who can listen to that without fear and without hurting their pious ears, and I continued to listen to someone's pious tenor reading out word for word the sentence for Albert Wollensky, son of Ferdinand and Ursula Wollensky, née Esch, whereby the jury took into account the legal proceedings, Mr. Wollensky, initiated against you by religious officials in defense resplendent faith and hope, as well as your repeated confessions, and decreed that the will of this court, which had God and the Holy Scriptures in its eyes and heart, must be executed in the name of the Father, of the Son, and of the Holy Spirit, amen, as we have established that your sister Tereza, a non-unbeliever, also honoring demons and surrendering to their blind forces, committed the most heinous crime by killing and eating her only son Adrian Novak, which all together deserved to be punished most severely and thus justice will be served as an example to others, we, Tereza, sentence you to be set to fire, blazed up and burnt from each and every side so that it leads to your death, for your soul to separate from your body and for your body to turn into ashes, heavenly sulfur, I shouted at the top of my lungs, having decided to throw something sharp at that tenor, with the serious intent of blinding him, and that's it, a spear miraculously appeared in my hand, but I threw it straight towards Tereza, which caused her to turn into a picture in which she was like a girl with a high, beautiful, extraordinary forehead into which the spear was driven and remained shaking for a while where its tip was stuck, and then I found out that the devil visited her before that, so when he asked her why she was sad, she answered that it was his fault that she had landed on her son's heart like a garden carpet moth and that she killed him at his persuasion, and the devil told her that he had no more power unless she hanged and suffocated, and she interestingly enough asked to be given a bag to make straps out of it, and she asked the devil where and from what to hang herself, to which he showed her an iron peg, stuck in the wall, and she hung herself on that peg with the intention to suffocate; the body swayed, and she would have probably been dead soon if I hadn't entered my dream and took her off half-dead, and then stripped her naked so that she wouldn't hang herself by her clothes, and afterwards I informed the judges about all this, so then they came and they questioned her once more, after which she confessed to them, crying, several other murders, which she had committed in a similar way, among other things, that she had killed several children in their mother's womb, and some while they were lying in the cradle, just by touching them, in the same manner she did with her Adrian, and when the children died and were buried, she unearthed them, taking them home and baking and eating them there...

I woke up with that not-at-all pleasant feeling.

XIV

LORD, WHO WILL LIVE WITHOUT FEAR? WHEN THEY MEET FACE TO FACE, FEAR OVERCOMES A MAN LIKE A SNAKE OVERCOMES A FROG. TO WHOM IS FEAR A GREATER DEITY: TO BRAVERY OR TO COWARDICE?

Today, the demon appeared in my dream again. It was the same with him as the previous night, but the icy, cold feeling when he descended into both my heads no longer caused pain, so I didn't wake up immediately. In any case, the very moment he touched me with his cold hand, I saw that I was indeed the two-headed one. I could move one head, while the other remained motionless. And that motionless one was actually me! The other one struggled to utter at least one word, which he somehow managed to do eventually, when he first gurgled some strange syllables like da-da, ma- ga-na, rainy, umbrellas, hangers, paper tissues, chipboard, women must not swear at God, steel-blue eyes of a lady- killer, gloomy Germanic mythology, people with frog eyes, and a book bound in rattlesnake skin.
- It's all the adjectives' fault. The only thing I'm guilty of is pronouncing them. For now, I have nothing else to state that might be of interest to you. Alev. Alev. Al. Al Capone, Alfi Kabiljo, Almirante, Altamira, Al Oerter, Albania. Al-al-al-al-la-la-la. Allah. Allahu akbar!

Why am I the one who grows two heads in my dream? The head serves a man only to be severed one day, just like a pumpkin.

My head is clear again. But it seems like it will soon burst if I think about the past night. It will be enough to say that I was drunk.

It was lukewarm and rainy. I must have crawled to my house on all fours; my muddy clothes attest to that.

When I found myself in the bedroom, I kicked the chair to hell because it got in my way in the dark. I somehow found the light switch. I saw the overturned chair in the middle of the room. I tried to undress. I managed somehow and stood proudly in front of the mirror.

I saw a miserable, pitiful, and dirty creature in front of me. The eyes oily and squinted.

A cold rage came over me; I puffed up and yelled at the top of my lungs at the man in the mirror: "Listen, you pig, standing there naked in front of me in the mirror, aren't you ashamed of what I see? Fall before me with that mirror and shatter into a thousand pieces!"

I raised my hand to strike him, but the one in the mirror also raised his hand to strike me. I was overcome with deep pity, and I sincerely told him: "Pull yourself together before it's too late. Do you realize that you cannot go on like this anymore?"

The one I addressed in the mirror also had tears flowing profusely from his eyes.

- It's fortunate that you have shown yourself to me today in your misery and stood before me. Wake up, my brother!

I don't even know how I got to bed. Soon, I fell asleep and started dreaming. The demons too arrived with me.

This time I dreamed of myself as a woman experiencing passionate love with the demon. But that love had a melodramatic ending; it didn't last long and didn't end happily.

I reached out to keep him with me a little longer, but I feel powerless to do anything to save that love. I'm despondent. Is it because of my suffering that I accept, it seems, too normally? A sweet longing overwhelms me, taking away any desire to work, to make any movement with my hand or foot. I feel like I am falling into a bottomless pit, feeling chills from the long fall, from which I will never emerge.

It occurs to me that I cannot seem to free myself from a strange infatuation with Tereza. This is something new for me. Until now, she was just a longing for me.

What does she know about me? What do I know about her? She is an odd person, both tough and soft, very sincere and speaks directly.

I'm not particularly handsome, but the most important thing is that I know what I want and how much I can do. My face is a bit gaunt, and I often blink. I think that's why I forget what I intend to say. When something angers me, I breathe deeply and grind my teeth, letting those near me know how dangerous it is to play carelessly with my nerves. I take my dose of sleeping pills every night.

How much time has passed since I last saw Arabella Herman, waving at her for so long, long, until the train disappeared around the bend, and my hand remained hanging in the air, my fingers still spread apart lifelessly. It was then that I first realized that a person cannot live without dreams. If someone had taken them away from me, I believe that I would have immediately taken my own life. As it was, everything got mixed up: the ugly woven into the beautiful, and the beautiful short and enchanting.

Is there anything more hypocritical than life past thirty? You decline and remember your hopes, which you might even sometimes sneer at, instead of looking at yourself in the mirror and saying: "You unfortunate phony!"

It was four in the morning, November fifteenth, nineteen seventy, Sunday was about to dawn. Cathérine Schmidt was driving the Citroën 2CV, and the two of us were sitting in the back seat. I knew we would soon part forever. I wanted to disintegrate right there, on the spot, in front of her, calling upon God, calling upon devils, but no one heeded me. She was speaking to me quietly and sleepily, saying I would make it to train because there was still half an hour, and we would be at the station in about ten minutes.

I wished that train would never arrive, nor that we would ever reach that lousy station, to steal at least a bit of time and be able to tell her a word or two: Arabella, if only you knew how much I love you; but there was no way to do it because of that lesbian behind the wheel who smoked like Humphrey Bogart and drove like Fangio, eagerly waiting to spit me out of the car and hand me over to the international train to Yugoslavia: Go with God's blessing, you and your language!

Arabella Herman. Arabella Herman. Where is she now, after eleven years, shemy Arabella Herman? Is she now in some Parisian suburb, waiting for her child in front of the school? Does she squat to the side to tie her child's untied shoelace? Does she sometimes sit at the kitchen table and think of me where am I? Is Arabella Herman even alive?

No one will ever love nor has anyone ever loved Arabella Herman as I have. Oh God, how can I believe that you alone have arranged this world? I hold a grudge against you for your ruthless indifference and intolerance towards those who suffer. Satan is more compassionate than you. I have never betrayed Arabella Herman in my heart, and whenever I think of her, I feel sympathy for my pain and longing. The devil is not as indifferent as you. You watch as your ant suffers, and you won't even reward its faith in you with a smile. All you know is how to avenge and extract capital from the unfortunate and miserable soul of man. No success can lessen the sorrow of pondering why you are like this with us. Perhaps it is because we believe in you out of sheer politeness, stupidity, or fear of future emptiness when we are mere dust and ashes. You use our disappointment, for which you undoubtedly have exceptional talent, to separate us from each other and diminish our joy in this dream of ours.

God, I always feel inferior before your name, and my rebellion has entirely human reasons to doubt your honorable intentions, in what you do with us. And yet, as a man with limited mind, but at the same time with a sense of pride, fear, and disdain for what torments me, I undoubtedly remain mute before your unapproachability and your mystically serious face while from your throne above, you watch, let's say, me as I now scornfully turn my nose up and wrestle with you like Jacob with the angel, requesting from you to finally grant me the most sublime omniscience so I would know and not just think that you do not exist and that you only needed to be invented to prevent the cognizance from nesting within us, the cognizance that we are alone, terribly alone, lonely, left to our own devices as we scratch in the ground on this planet like chickens. You stand between our loneliness and our conceit, and you will always stand to be a comfort to the former and a warning to the latter.

Look, what an irony of your existence; a sufficient reason for me to agree that we must not banish you from our minds, of course, excluding those who blaspheme you, place everything beautiful and human underfoot, and those who resist indoctrinated consciousness.

In your "existence", there is something unusual: it takes a lot of melancholy and self-loathing to satisfy your demands. Such flirtation is achieved by both sweetness and tenderness in the soul, which only explains your seductiveness and audacity to exploit it before us. Both in joy and in doubt, the heart will undoubtedly be solitary. Then only your voice is still warm.

God, have you ever been ashamed that you even came up with the crazy idea of creating this world for your own fiefdom, to have someone to threaten with doom? Is it really worth threatening the one who knows he is already doomed the moment his heart first stirred in his mother's womb? This is your idiotic idea for us to gnaw through the shell around us and slip into your world, and that you initially enchant us with illusions, so that we could mock them later. Only the smart and the devils go their own way.

XV

WELL, EVERYONE IS ALLOWED TO BE BLESSED IN THEIR OWN WAY, ESPECIALLY BETWEEN TWO SINS, TWO LAWS, TWO PUNISHMENTS, TWO SUFFERINGS

To this day, it's not entirely clear to me why I didn't think about writing as much as such a challenge requires, a challenge that needed to be accepted, primarily out of vanity, inasmuch as it is considered a stimulus for vanity. But even now I think that I managed to completely exclude vanity from that process, of course, I say again if thereby we don't mean the writer's normal desire to eventually have what he has written see the light.

The risk was huge, but I have always loved dangers. In writing, there are no favorites, and a beginner can have a certain advantage over a Nobel Prize winner; moreover, I believe that a Nobel laureate only has the advantage of their authority, which can be yet another obstacle; otherwise, everything else is on the side of the one who has nothing to lose. Imagine the advantage you have when you cannot lose anything because your lack of obligation gives you that right. The one who, for instance, can write whatever he wants without being taken amiss, just as everyone will eagerly scrutinize an established authority and look for the tiniest faults.

The risk grew day by day, and this helped me stay in shape and dive even deeper into writing, which had already become breathing.

Gradually, I imagined my characters more and more, and it was nice to be in their shoes. A writer's brain needs to learn to serve a craft that is akin to martyrdom. As for loneliness, let's not even talk about it right now.

Woe is me! As soon as I first announced that I was placing writing above all else, I immediately heard my father's assessment that I would be the one to completely degrade and bring to rotting branches, if not to a stump, such a magnificent and rich tree that few families possess. My decision would ultimately once and for all distance the family from the planned and dreamed paths it was supposed to follow; and it comes from meon whom the greatest hopes were set. Had I said that I intended to clean streets in the future, it wouldn't have caused as much commotion as when I said that I would write stories.

- *So vat?*heard him lecturing Tereza in the next room *I also know how to tell stories, but it never occurred to me to write them. I'd put a plow in zee hands of all such people, and they'd talk less.*

Tereza was silent, I knew she didn't know whose side to take. She couldn't side with my father without hurting me, nor could she side with me without even more offending my father.

When I soon finished my first novel, I couldn't help but share the news with them.

I won't talk about the content of the novel. However, I must immediately emphasize that I noticed from their faces that they liked the story because they managed to identify most of the characters in the book with some people they themselves knew. Father had the opportunity to observe up close the man who was my main character. The way I described him, told his fate, and also how I led him from situation to situation delighted my father so much that he completely forgot himself, laughing heartily at my devilish observations of the character, and his caution and reserve about what I was writing slipped his mind. That old fox still harbored hope that I wasn't talented for such things and that I would return to education and teaching children instead of remaining a sort of scribbler and pen-pusher. Once, without a single word, he entered my room just to shove a piece of paper under my nose, listing writers who died of tuberculosis before they turned thirty: "*Zey are all TPC!*"[2] He then winked at me in confidence, whispering to me so that apparently no one would hear us.

Now I say father lost all caution and was laughing freely with his bleating voice. The old fox recognized the main character, whom I had kept hidden under a different surname but whose life exactly matched the life of a man he knew up close and whose life paths had once intersected way too much.

When it came to the character embodying charm and goodness, and the cursed victim of the first one, my father was all ears because he immediately recognized himself.

I didn't intend to try to rehabilitate him with the book, nor did I want it to be a kind of documentary novel; rather, I wanted to use history as material for a complex melodrama about justice, crime, and betrayal.

Was I right in seeing my father as a total victim carried away by his idealism? Was his suffering hasty, making it seem like a true children's picture book? Although I am a man who was born after the last war and remember the events from the book less than I could recall some of them through a fog, I cannot claim to be reliable when writing about that period. I think I was too pathetic.

My father was sympathetic to the story, though he immediately let me know a few of his objections. They mainly concerned his character in the novel: that he had not in the slightest lost enthusiasm for the revolution that even "*today ineksorably continues*". When he said "*ineksorably*", he joined his two thistle-like eyebrows, raised his finger in the air, and it was immediately clear to Tereza that this was also the beginning of a lesson in political economy, as well as in dialectical and historical materialism.

- *How musch will ya get for zis?*he asked me in the end.
- I don't know I replied nor does it matter. My greatest reward is the satisfaction I felt while writing.

---

[2] TPC = TBCabbreviation for tuberculosis (Eng. TB)

He grabbed his chin. I could see he had something important to tell me.

- *Listen, zat sing about TPC mostly applies to zee nineteens century, zere's a little bit of it in zee twenties century, but very little, better to saynosing! I read somevere zat Hesse vas a banker, Kafka vas in an inshurance company, Andrić in diplomacy... on one side, a decent okupation, and when ya come home, ya eat vell, rest a bit, and work on your ovn stuff as much as ya vant. On one side, every first of zee month zee state guarantees ya a salary, if ya wantentertain yerself, if ya don'tdon't even entertain yerself. Do as ya please.*

I am thirty years, four months, and eleven days old. Tereza is exactly two years and nine days older than me. Although she wasn't beautiful, she attracted with her charm; she resembled our father in her facial features. Until the age of twenty-five, she was thin, but then suddenly, as if something strange happened to her: she began to gain weight rapidly. I would be too naive if I explained it primarily by her divorce orby the fact that she discovered that her little Adrian reacted abnormally to things around him.

She fought against the weight gain until she reached a hundred kilos, but when she apparently realized that there was no point in fighting it, she completely gave up and, it seems, surrendered to gluttony. Her neck was covered in fat, and her arms couldn't hang vertically from her shoulders. Her two tiny eyes looked sadly behind thick glasses. I didn't know where to look, and my gaze usually stopped at the dimples at the base of each finger. Then I couldn't think of anything nice to say to her. It all seemed stupid and unnecessary, so I preferred to stay silent and wait for her to ask me something. Since she also remained silent, I assumed that the same thoughts were running through her head. All I could do was to smile at her. She smiled back at me.

She touched her damp, red face with a large white handkerchief and turned towards the window. I was standing behind her and watching how huge her back was, and beneath the robe, her thick

pink legs. She was all ruddy. The smell of her sweat filled the room. A strange thought came to my mind that I shouldn't breathe this air too much because I might become fat too.
- Today is the anniversary of mom's death she snorted, turning to look directly at me with those fish-like eyes.
- I know I replied. I saw her today on the street in that blue muslin dress of hers. She just waved at me. Oh, I almost forgot: she also smiled at me.
- You're in a babbling mood today she noted. Otherwise, you don't talk much, do you?

It was obvious that she was reproaching me for reminding her of mom more than convention and bourgeois morality would allow. Her eyes were still watching me and it seemed to me that she was bothered by a headache, which was a sign of her nervous suffering because of my indiscreet reminder of mother, which was bound to soon move and excite me as well.

Actually, I felt quite comical when I entered her room long ago, while she was still married to Emil Novak. The two of them were sleeping in bed. Tereza was lying on her back with her arm stretched out, and Emil, pressed against her side, was lying on her arm. They had nothing on, and the sheet reached only up to their waists.

I stood at the foot of the bed for a long time and observed them. I felt as if I had discovered some secret. Then Tereza opened her eyes, saw me staring at her and *a certain spot*, and gestured with her hand for me to leave the room.

Does she still remember that event? Does she wonder where Emil is, as I wonder where Arabella Herman is?

Tereza doesn't like to cook, but she is always there when it comes to baking cakes. While baking them, she loves to scoop a bit of cream with her fingertip and stick her finger in her mouth. It seems to me that she always experienced ecstasy at that moment.

I was always sad whenever I saw that. At such moments, I would think that she lived only for suffering and food. It took her quite some time to prevent and reason with Adrian not to stick his fingers into the hot oven and not to put the knife with cream in his mouth. It was even harder to stop him from knocking pots of boiling milk off the stove.

Suddenly, I wished to take Tereza and Adrian to the river in the afternoon, to go for a boat ride.

It was late last night, after long thoughts about the fate of my sister Tereza Wollensky and the transience of all hope and things, that I got up from the table to leave the closer examination of her personality for one of the following days. I went to bed. Obviously, the thought of her haunted me in my sleep. In any case, I don't remember ever having such a dream as I did that night. The demons reappeared.

With that not-at-all pleasant feeling, I woke up drenched in sweat.

XVI

MAN IS INCAPABLE OF BEING EVEN PERMANENTLY UNHAPPY. AFTER ALL, EVERYONE SHUTS IN WITH THEIR OWN DOOR

Albert Wollensky had kept his demons locked inside himself for ten years. In good weather, it was less painful because he could take out the sunlounger and stretch out in the sun in the garden in front of the house.

On Wednesday, June 19th, his father visited him around ten in the morning. They exchanged a few words, each from their side of the fence. They parted. Albert Wollensky stretched out in the garden. The weather was nice. A gentle breeze was pushing the white clouds.

Suddenly, he got up, went into the house, took a box of bullets and a carbine he had bought a few years earlier, put them in the trunk of the car, opened the gate, and ran out into the street.

First, he went to his parents' house. He looked for his father. He wasn't there. No matter, he would go to his uncle's. They talked, and then his uncle brought a ladder and climbed onto the cherry tree. Albert went to the car, opened the trunk, took out the carbine, and shot the man in the tree three times.

From there, he returned to his father's house. His father still wasn't there. With the rifle in hand, he entered the kitchen and fired a shot at Eva Tvrdi, the cook, just as she turned to tell him that it wasn't time for lunch yet. Just one bullet, which grazed her skull. As if nothing had happened, he told her: "I'll be back."

He went to the center of the little town, to the local square, to Doctor Flaker's office. He found no one there. He passed through the house and entered the office. There he found the doctor talking with a patient. He calmly aimed the carbine at the doctor's head and fired twice.

The killer calmly returned to the car, put the carbine in the trunk, and headed towards his parents' house. There he found his father in front of the house and killed him. Then he passed through the house and entered the bedroom of Tereza Wollensky, his sister, who at that moment was bent over her son Adrian, a twelve-year-old boy, retarded since birth. Four bullets into her back and two into the boy's head.

At the end of this massacre, the killer entered the living room, went to the piano, and played Beethoven's "Für Elise".

The killing spree continued. Albert Wollensky's demons had been unleashed. Now he was shooting at everyone he met on the street. Always the same scenario: he would stop the car, take the carbine out of the trunk, kill, put the weapon back in the trunk, and continue on his way. First, he killed two men, then another, and then another, continuing his killing spree with a housewife and ending his madness with a truck driver who was just waiting with his truck to turn onto the main road.

When the police finally arrived, he got out of the car with his hands up. He only said: "Don't shoot! I'm sick! And one more thing my last name is spelled with a double-u, a double-l, and make sure to end it with a wye."

- Oh, that means you are of noble origin...?!remarked the inspector.

The killer beamed with joy.

- Yes!

While the inspector was writing the ending "wye", he asked him by mimic "is that so?" "is it all right?", and the killer, very happy, proud, elegantly and aristocratically bowed.

By psychiatric observations in the course of treatment it was established that his personality was of a simpler structure with obsessive traits, introverted, shy in the interpersonal communication, of a higher educational level and intellectual abilities. The available data and psychiatric findings indicated that before the traumatic event, he did not exhibit signs of manifest mental disorders in terms of mental illnesses, organic diseases of the nervous system, or sexual deviations.

The patient's current condition is significantly better than before, but he complains of headaches and dizziness, and shows signs of depression.

The doctors suggest that because of this, he requires supervision by other persons until an optimal situation is created in which he will feel protected and safe, and only then can he be brought before the court.

As for his attitude towards art, he is like the sorcerer's apprentice, a doubting apprentice who does not understand the secrets of the craft. He had brought to life the demons over which he lost control. He is a doubly fake artist; too arrogant and too submissive towards life.

I CANNOT CLAIM WHEN YOU ARE ON YOUR OWN, WHEN YOU ARE LEFT AT THE MERCY OF YOUR OWN SELF, WHEN YOU ARE ALONE WITH YOURSELF, THAT IT IS IN EVERY WAY TERRIFYING, BUT IT IS ONE OF

THE CRAZIEST ADVENTURES IN THIS WORLD: TO MEET YOUR OWN SELF...

I could never have imagined that just a few moments later, such a feeling of complete abandonment could be provoked in the human heart. The sound I had never heard before: the rustle of blood in my own ears now engulfed me like the beating of sea waves in the midst of solitude.

I am ending my story here. I admit that I do this almost with some resistance. I put the pen down. I feel somehow strange. Already now, I cannot honestly say whether, in fact, I remember some observations correctly and accurately, or should I judge them as mere hallucinations in the form of shadows of experiences.